Also By Joseph Christy

Brief Interruptions

Doolittle Proxy

Tales From The Bone Yard: The Bog

Monks of Shel

josephbchristy.com

Also By Matt Christy

Mad Fits and Half Starts

Limestone

Mama Will Hold You

TRIBUTARIES

Joseph Christy & Matt Christy

Cover design by Matt Christy

Interior illustrations by Joseph Christy

Edited by Amethyst Stark

Printed by Palimpsest Independent Publishing

First Printing Edition, 2022

ISBN 979-8-9873228-0-2

Tributaries

ACT ONE

October 1987

I mean they come outta nowhere. Great dizzying clouds of em. All of Iron County was infested with gypsy moths. About the size of quarter. Hit so many with the truck I could scoop 'em off my windshield in handfuls. They was everywhere. They was something awful in the trees. Hundreds of old oaks died. I mean, for weeks it was hell. Folks was still cleanin 'em out of fans and vents for years. This local preacher, young fella, walked up through town with a bell and a Bible calling it "the end times". Fancied himself the town prophet, I guess. When they swarmed at night, sometimes covering the street lights whole, this ole son of a bitch would stand on the corner of 3rd and Vernon calling out, "Repent, the land is swarmed by our sins! Repent, the kingdom is at hand!" That same ole apocalyptic message that's been around since damn near all civilization. Standing there with all them moths spinning about him. T'was a sight. I heard he died of a snake bite preachin' the gospel out near Coalton. I don't know much about it, except it gave me a new respect for him. I figure a man that worships with venomous snakes, might be a true believer. Anyway, a week later, poof, moths vanished. Just up and gone. Thought maybe they all just died. Short lifespans, you know. But you know these people. Everyone had their theory. Conspiracies popped up everywhere. That preacher got a write-up on the front page of the Tribune calling it "The Grace of God"; week after, a farmer wrote a response, got tucked in letters to the editor, said a late frost was coming and they went south. Just moved on. Hell, I don't know, maybe those is the same thing.

1

A kettle of turkey vultures stirred the clouds above the treeline as he drove the backcountry. Winding his way deeper into these Ohio hills. He slowed down to a crawl. Ellis Road. The Bronco inched forward the way one might creep along a cemetery at night. Sunlight fell dappled through the trees onto the gravel road. JJ had hiked, four-wheeled, and driven up most of them. Some as a boy hunting with his father, some as a fisherman, and some as an Officer of the State. The dark alley of roadway gave way to a wall of green and JJ smashed the gas and drove fast with his fingertips cutting through the windstream. The scent of the honeysuckle underbrush dense in the ditches.

The Bronco tires on the driveway woke a dog. A barrel shaped slobbering mutt that ran around the truck and barked at the back tires.

A woman carrying a toddler on her hip leaned out the screen door of a small trailer and stared down at him from her porch with that blunt meanness that seemed to mark the members of the Kindred family.

"Vicki!" she shouted at the mutt. "Hush!"

The bottom half of the white trailer was speckled with a vomity green mold from the wet Ohio spring.

JJ rolled down his window and forced a smile at her.

"How do, Sarah," he nodded.

She raised her leg and swatted at a fly on her calf.

"Hi," she said. "Vicki, shut up," she said to her dog.

The baby stared at JJ with its soft, blank-eye grin.

"I'm headed on up to see Junior."

Her eyes were red-rimmed and dark and they scuttled over JJ and the truck. She leaned over the railing and squint in the windows of the truck. She said, "Bullet," then turned her attention to the dogs and yelled at them again.

"Sorry?" JJ said.

She pointed up the hill and waved him on.

With the dog announcing his arrival, he pulled up at the foot of a low-lying log cabin that was flanked by two giant oaks. A brand new Dodge Viper sat there, low lying, sexy, sculpted for speed. Its blue body shined in the sun.

The Kindred property wore a series of half-collapsed shacks and sheds, a rusted out motorcycle engine lay in front of the cabin next to a stack of firewood, two stripped cars a little further on, an old Chrysler sedan and a Jeep with no tires, a maple sapling growing in the passenger seat. An Airstream trailer rusted completely orange lay next to a school portable so overgrown with Virginia creeper that it was hard to tell where the entrance was.

The blue Viper shined sleek and catlike with its missile elegance and grooved gills, ultramarine with white racing stripes down the hood. He turned the Bronco off and put his aviators on. A teenage boy in a tattered Metallica shirt and overalls stood on the top of the rise near one of the shacks with a rifle slung over his shoulder staring at JJ. He stepped out of the truck and raised a hand to the boy but he didn't move. Vicki came to him barking and jumping. He took the dog by it's hind legs and looked in it's watering eyes and enormous tongue. The boy yelled and the dog went running for him.

JJ turned to the cabin that sat squat and dark under large green boughs. He wore the tan-colored Fish and Wildlife shirt with the badge of the jumping fish and the flying mallard on the chest pocket and the regulation pants with the dark green stripes. He walked past the sculpture-turned-lawn-ornament of a smiling, bronze buddha, brown rainwater in the barrel of the arms where cigarette butts swam. On the tiny porch, a toddler in diapers pushed a plastic lawn mower that clanged as it rolled.

"Hey, little guy, your daddy home?"

It stood dumb, looking up at him, and grumbled something like words.

The door clacked open. "Forte, it's about damn time you got here. I've been calling your office all morning, man." He turned and yelled back in the house, "Hey, I got the Game Warden out here. Finish that up." He stepped his bare feet into a pair of boots, then motioned for JJ to follow, rubbing the toddler's head as he clomped down the steps. His face was thorny and angular and his ponytail sat wrapped in a topknot on his head like a coiled rope. His arms were covered over in a lace of blue-black tattoo flames. Vicki, escaped her captor, came round the corner of the cabin and came up to the men wagging her tail.

"So what's up, Junior?" JJ asked, eyeing the dog.

"Bullet."

"What?"

"It's Bullet now. No more Junior."

JJ touched a scabbed wound above the dog's eye and recoiled.

Bullet clapped at the animal, "Get on home, you fat bitch." And the dog stopped and back stepped looking up at Bullet, its jowls wagging. "Watched this dog ate its own last spring and Fran was pissed, lord. Ate three puppies in the same hour. Liked it, didn't ya? Hungry, mean, my god, mean dog. Go home, Vicki!"

The dog sat down and licked its gray tit-covered belly.

"What's with the kid?" JJ asked, nodding at the teenager standing sentinel in the distance with his gun.

"Don't worry 'bout Karl; that's a good boy," Bullet said, then turned towards the boy and yelled, "Don't shoot the game warden, Karl!"

The kid jerked his chin up in acknowledgement and watched them walk the field. They crossed between two small cabins made of grey wood slats with corrugated metal roofs. Junior stepped over a braid of extension cords that passed from one window to the other. A neon Budweiser sign glowed on a wall inside one of the dark rooms.

"We all a bit jumpy right now, Forte."

Rounding the side of another mobile home they entered a haller that touched the edge of the woods.

"Where we going, Junior?"

Junior looked back and said with a finger on each syllable, "Bull-et."

A deer path led through the high yellowed grasses and they were met with a hot rotten smell like hog shit. Bullet stepped aside to let JJ see a spotted blue tick in the grass at the edge of the trees, its belly ripped out and blood strung along the ground where it had been dragged.

"Jesus Christ." The viscera covered in buzzing green bottle flies.

Bullet stood with his hand on his chin, looking sad. Part of its flesh chewed up, missing the lower jaw, the flies busy at the coagulated blood.

"I loved that dumb dog."

JJ backed away.

"That ain't all. Come on."

JJ followed him up in the woods where there laid another one with its eyes gone.

"Found some innards up in that tree."

"Lord." JJ squatted to look in the empty sockets.

"Come on, I gotta show ya everything."

The third dog lay to the West covered over by tall wheatgrass. Sliced to the bone by claws or teeth.

"No bullet wounds or anything."

"Nope. Buzzards already been at 'em. Maggie was headed out huntin' turkey yesterday mornin' and saw Toenail lying like he is, came in screaming at me."

"What do you think it was?"

Bullet looked at JJ. "Well shit, yer the detective."

A little stringy bit of dog flesh hung in the hooked burrs of a burdock bulb.

"I tell ya, these weren't no pussy dogs."

JJ studied the depressions in the dewy grass and looked for tracks in the dirt. A mossy log lay on the ground and he eyed the wood, kneeled to look at the oxidation on a snapped branch to see if he could calculate time of it's breaking, a darker coloration suggesting an older break. He knew some of the questions to ask and he knew the evidence lay in the environment. What was the weight of the breaker? In which direction were they headed? But to interpret the signs accurately with the old Native tracking techniques took years of experience he didn't have, stuck most days behind a desk or a car. He found a good set of dog prints. The edge of Bullet's own boot.

"We can throw up some bear traps. Maybe put some human hair and other animals' scents around if y'all're worried," JJ said, following Bullet back towards the cabin.

Inside the mobile home, a curtain moved. Jack Kindred's large, white leathery face stared at them from the darkened window.

Bullet shrugged. "Hell JJ, we got enough guns and bodies round here to repel a pack of wolves. That'n first one we come ta was Daddy's favorite purebred."

JJ looked up at the now empty window. "How's the old man?"

Bullet looked at the window, too. "Ah, got'em a cold." Bullet walked to the front door and held up his hand. "You give me a second."

The trailer's lower foundations were built up on cinder blocks and old car wheels. A giant TV antenna shot up silver among the golden green of the trees. JJ took his sweaty ball cap off and ran his hands through his dark, oily hair. The heat gathered the humidity in the holler so you could sweat just standing there. He looked back at the field where the dogs lay.

Bullet came out the glass door carrying a brown paper sack. The towering Jack Kindred followed, waving at JJ with a huge smile.

"How you holding up, son?" said the old man in his wheezing voice, a bit stooped with age and with a slight limp in his left leg but colossal in his size, hands impressively large, farmhandle rough, dirt under thick fingernails.

"I'm alright, Mr. Kindred. I'm alright."

"We all liked your daddy fine."

"Thank you, sir."

"How long's it been since you've been running the shop?"

"It's been two years now."

"Has it been that long?"

"Yessir."

"My, my, time runs on like a watched kettle."

"Here," Bullet said, offering him the bag.

JJ hesitated.

"You gonna take it?"

Kindred Sr. paid no mind to the boys looking off at the woods with watery gunmetal eyes, his white hair slicked back. An angry tattooed tiger down one freckled hairy arm coming out his black t-shirt.

"Could we do this in my truck next time?" said JJ.

The old man turned his attention on JJ. Father and son exchanged a brief glance.

Bullet laughed, "You don't gotta be worried, bud. Ain't no one 'round."

JJ took the paper sack and tucked it in his shirt.

"That was my dog, you know?" said the huge man.

"Yeah, I'm sorry."

Jack grinned. They stood there watching each other with the red eyed cicadas droning unseen in the woods and the dog bodies rotting in the rising heat.

Overhead fluorescents bathed the office in a sterile brightness. Cardboard boxes with case files that stretched back to the '70s sat on a wooden filing cabinet. A sticker of the seal of Ohio on one of the double glass doors cast a shadow on the blue tile floor. JJ squeaked the front door open rifling through the mail with both hands.

Donna sat at her desk with a computer and CB radio and a telephone and behind her grew a bird of paradise in a pot. She wore her glasses a little low on her nose and almost never raised her voice or was in a hurry. She was packing a stack of newspapers into a beer box and said, "JJ, we need any of these old newspapers?"

Morning light fell in slatted stripes on her desk.

"No."

"What about this?"

She opened the flaps on a box full of plastic trophies. JJ took one out.

"Dad's Skeet awards."

"Yeah."

"He won, what, ten years in a row?"

"Yep, he weren't shy about saying so either."

"No, I guess he wasn't." The little plastic gold man with an aimed rifle stood on a chalice. "Toss'em out."

"They's so many."

"I know."

"I thought we canceled our subscription to 'Wild Country'?" He said holding up a magazine with a moose on it.

"I thought I did."

"Well, do it again?"

"Yup."

"Look at that, got a coupon for pork loin. Need that?"

"No."

He dropped the mail in the trash and opened his office.

"How were the Kindreds?" asked Donna. "Was it a mean coyote?"

JJ stood at the door of his office shaking his head scratching absently at the peeling paint on the metal doorway.

"If it was a coyote, it was the Charles Manson of coyotes," he said.

JJ went into his office and closed the door shut behind him. The air conditioner clicked off and a heavy silence hung in the room. Brown leather-bound law books with their gold dates on the spines lining the walls. Mounted above his heavy mahogany desk was a large framed photograph of a man in a cowboy hat looking at the camera smiling, wearing the beige fish and wildlife uniform from the seventies and in gold at the bottom of the photograph the man's name, James J. Forte Sr. Everywhere his father was still evident in the office. His coffee mugs and his shot glasses in the kitchen and his gun and bow mounted on the wall and the smell of his cigarettes still in the desk and in the walls and even in the drooping fern that hung from a hook in the ceiling tile.

He moved a box on the filing cabinet under the window and slid his hand in the crack and pulled out a key taped to the back of the cabinet and rolled the key in his finger, listening for Donna outside his door and then sat at his desk and unlocked the bottom drawer. Inside sat stacks of paper bags folded up and rubberbanded. He pulled the sack from his jacket pocket and opened it and took a handwritten note from it and put it on his desk.

The note read: *Stay off Ellis.*

It was one of a handful identical notes in identical paper sacks he'd received since inheriting the job.

Rain began to fall in great sudden sheets on his window. He ran his thumb through the fifty-dollar bills and rubber-banded them together and dropped it in with the others and closed it shut.

Novak backed out of the rain into the office with a plastic coffee mug in one hand and a newspaper covering his head with the other. He stuffed the soggy paper into the trashcan and set his cup on Donna's desk.

"Really coming down out there," he said and he took off his green rain slicker and shook it, giving Donna a jolt of cold water. Her glasses covered in beads. "Ernie!"

He hooked the coat on the rack by the door.

"Oh, sorry, Miss Donna."

JJ peeked through the wooden blinds and tucked the note in his pocket.

She rubbed her glasses on her blouse with both hands giving Ernie a death stare.

Novak heavy set, wide in the middle and wider still with his big policeman's belt, the gun and the huge flashlight, did an exaggerated bow with a flourish of his hands, and said in a trumped up impression of southern aristocracy. "My deepest apologies your highness." He put one hand on her desk and smiled. "Why don'tcha let me make it up to ya? We could take a boat out on the lake, bring some wine coolers…"

"Ernie, shut up," Donna said.

"Miss Donna, yer breaking my heart." Still in his theatrics, putting a hand to his chest and leaning his head back.

He grinned, grabbed his coffee, and walked into JJ's office without knocking. JJ sat reading a small black and white magazine. He did not look up but said, "She's gonna get you back one day, Novak."

"She likes me," he said loud enough so Donna could hear.

JJ lowered the magazine. "She's a married woman, Ernie."

"Yeah, for how long now, Donna?"

"Eight years," Donna said, patting her desk dry with a paper towel.

"Eight years. She's bored out of her mind. What d'yall do it once a week, every other week...once a month?"

Donna shook her head.

"So Ernie, what brings ya down?"

"Do I need a reason to come see my buddy? I thought you were gonna clean this place up." Novak slid a finger down his dusty bookcase and looked disgusted at his dirty finger, held it up for JJ to see.

"We're working on it," Donna said.

"You've been saying that for years. I don't see how you find nothing in here, Forte. I believe it's worse than when your old man was running the place."

JJ shuffled a stack of manila folders together and put them in a box.

"We're finally making a dent in the stacks. Dad left the place an absolute mess. Thirty years of mishandled paperwork."

Novak slid a folder out at random and flipped it open.

"What is this stuff anyhow?"

"Old case files. Ernie, I just got some of this in order."

A picture fell from the folder and Novak scooped it off the floor.

"Woa!" said Novak and held it up for JJ to see.

A dead lion stretched out on a police cruiser. Behind the domed lights a row of white houses close together, a mailbox and a maple tree.

JJ took the photo and studied quietly for a moment.

"I remember him telling me about this."

"Yeah? You're old man killed a lion?"

"No. No, I don't think he's the one shot it. Some rich guy's private zoo let loose in the suburbs. A wild story."

On JJ's desk was a framed photo of JJ Sr. and Uncle Glen kneeling and holding the legs of an enormous dead turkey grinning with self satisfaction up at the photographer. Novak sat and picked up the photo.

"Your old man did some shit."

JJ said, "Biggest wild turkey ever recorded in Ohio. That's a forty pound turkey."

"Forte, you tell me that every goddamn time I'm in here."

"Ernie, you're bothering me, what do you want?"

"Oh, I'm just here to flirt with Miss Flanders."

"I can hear you," Donna said from her desk. Ernie winked at JJ.

"Ernie."

"Alright, calm down. You haven't talked to Jack Kindred lately, have ya?"

"I just got back from there."

"I got a message from Jack Junior."

"What's he saying?"

"Something about a bear or a serial killer, hell, I don't think Louise knew what to do with him."

"Bullet."

"Oh right, Bullet." Ernie laughed.

"Someone or something slaughtered three of their dogs."

"Damn, sorry I missed that."

"No, you ain't."

"I was out on the river. Had me a lady friend."

Ernie leaned back to see if Donna was at her desk but she was up watering the plants in the foyer.

He leaned in and said in a low voice, "Best investment I ever made, JJ. I get more pussy with this boat than I ever did on land. Might consider getting ya one."

"I'll keep that in mind."

Novak tapped JJ's desk with his fingers.

"So Junior told ya his name is Bullet now, huh? Fuckers crazy as a river rat."

JJ slipped the folder back in it's place and slipped the cardboard lid on the box.

"Did he tell ya why?" Ernie asked.

"Why he's crazy? I think that's genetics."

JJ with a sharpie labeling the box with a year and a month.

"Why he's calling himself Bullet?"

"Didn't ask."

"Well, get this here, so, Junior goes out hunting one morning along Dominic Ridge. Last deer season he tells me, but I doubt that, you know. You know where that is?"

"Yeah. Over by the..."

"Yeah, yeah, he was out there and was, according to this jackass, alone stalking this huge albino buck. You imagine this nimrod stalking anything smelling like Joe Camel? You seen these albino deer?"

"Yeah, I seen them. Nelson's got a picture on his desk. It's pretty good."

"I'd love a white buck bastard on my mantle. Anyhow, Bullshit, I mean, Bullet, sees it up on the ridge. You know, he talks real epic about it. These hunters... And he shoots it. Bang. Bang. Two shots, right in a row. Double-tap. Then he runs after it cause it bolts. He runs it down and finds it thrashing in some leaves. Huge. He tells me he waits on it to die. Didn't want to put any more holes in it cause he was getting it mounted. Alright, so he drags the thing back to his truck, alone, like this skinny little bitch could've drug out that big buck, anyways and he starts looking for the kill shots. But he can only find one but he knows he hit it twice. So, he digs out the bullet. But he don't just dig out one, he finds both of them in the same hole. Robin Hooded the thing. Now, what are the odds this is real? I don't know. But I did see the mount. Twelve pointer. I'd say it'd score over hundred fifty. Hanging in his trailer it takes up the whole wall."

"I don't believe it."

"Something's off about it right?"

"Something's off with all of them."

"Yeah. Well, don't say that too loud. That old tycoon may well be mayor before we know it."

"God."

"Or worse yet, we'll be answering to Mister Bullet hisself." Ernie said, rapping his knuckles on the only clear corner of JJ's desk as he stood to leave. "I gotta take a leak. I gotta take a leak, Donna," he said walking past Donna's desk and heading down the hallway. Donna shook her head.

JJ took the box and stacked it with the others in the corner of his office.

When Novak came back he paused at JJ's office door with a weird look and backed up and JJ watched him back down the hallway to study their bulletin board.

"Hoe-lee shit."

JJ put both his hands through his hair and pulled them down his face. "Ernie, I got shit to do."

"Just a second, Forte. Just a second."

On the bulletin board, UFO sightings were plotted with red thumbtacks on a huge map of southeast Ohio. Newspaper clippings, one of a big fish with feet like flippers, an enormous dead octopus that was pulled out of the Ohio River, blurry images of trees with red circles drawn around abstract shapes, a few images with dark spots on the crisscrossed trusses.

"This must be your detective Nelson's?"

"Leave it alone, Ernie."

"No, no, no, this is some amazing work, JJ. I mean this is real sleuthing. Don't you think, Donna? I mean your guy is really plugged in, ear to the ground, nose to the grind."

"Leave it, Ernie."

"Oh, Jesus. You guys are funny. Donna, you know where I'll be if you need me, honey."

As Ernie was walking past Nelson's desk, he saw the photo of the albino deer, picked it up, and looked back at JJ.

"Damn nice picture," he said and put it down. The front door shut behind him, and JJ stood staring at the bulletin board his fingers interlaced behind his head. The only sound was Donna at the copy machine, the arm buzzing back and forth in its glass box.

Finally, Donna said, "You ain't taking him seriously are ya?"

"He ain't wrong, Donna. I outta ask Nelson to take this crap down."

"Nelson's harmless."

"I know it."

"And he's dependable."

"Yeah, yeah, yeah..."

The three men stood in the rain a little dejected, the dead canine carcass at their feet. Bullet held his toddler in one arm. The boy fiddled with a toy gun. Nelson, a thin clean shaven young man, hair a little wiry, brown with just a touch of red in it, held his hand up to the raindrops and looked at the sky.

"He takes a better picture than I do," JJ said to Bullet and nodded over at Nelson.

Bullet shook his head and looked Nelson's thin body up and down, a little disgruntled by the young man's appearance on his land.

"I'll take excellent pictures, Mr. Bullet."

Nelson flipped his tripod open and scrolled the legs out and set it in the grass.

"I'm gonna take another look at the tracks yonder," said JJ. "Check the fanny pack, Nelson."

Nelson hitched his camera to the tripod and looked up, said, "What?"

"Don't you be wondering far now," Bullet said.

The wind picked up and tore at the trees. A gray low lying sky spit rain irregular. JJ pointed at his belt and said, "Fanny pack," to Nelson.

Nelson unfolded an umbrella and it caught in the wind and he nearly toppled the camera right into the blood and viscera. JJ walked into the woods.

"Mind holding this for me, Mr. Bullet?" Bullet and the child looked at him with the same bland expression. "Be mighty helpful if ya did."

Reluctantly, Bullet took it. The boy reached out and grabbed the umbrella handle too. Nelson bent and leveled the lens at the dead dog and focused the camera and pressed the button and realized he had no film. He unlatched the camera and then felt in his pockets and then the pack on his belly. He unzipped his fanny pack and pulled a canister and thread the film into the camera. Bullet tracked JJ's movement a little ways up the hill and then turned his attention to the gangly photographer.

Nelson said, "Could have been a bear."

"Yep," said Bullet.

"But you think it was a wolf?"

He looked dead pan at the man.

"Yep."

"A wolf pack?"

"Might."

"Could have been coyotes maybe."

Bullet paused a moment and spat and said, "Yep."

The boy leaned in his father's arms to look down at the massacred dog and Nelson watched him.

"You sure you want your boy seeing all this?"

Bullet looked at Nelson and spat again and said, "Yep."

He took a picture of the blue tick's ruptured neck and twisted the film. Turkey vultures circled above the tree line and the little boy pointed his gun at them and snapped the trigger. Pop pop.

Nelson stood. "Maybe it ain't professional of me to comment, as you're currently in mourning about your pets. However, I'm of the mind that this could have been perpetrated by something of a more sinister, more mysterious nature."

Bullet eyed Nelson. Rain dripping from the umbrella.

"Why just look at the way they were cut from one end to the other? What animal would do that? Do wolves do that?"

"Cut the shit out of them."

Nelson looked at the child. "Ah, ah," said Nelson and pointed to the boy, "you're parrot's listening, Mr. Bullet. I'm sure you would agree, one's gotta be careful not to introduce the young to the wicked ways of the world too soon on account of our doings and sayings."

"His name's Goat. And he don't talk."

Nelson watched the boy pick his nose.

A path cut through the woods and JJ found deer tracks there. He wasn't sure what he was looking for but he let himself go quiet and observe. He remembers his father saying it to him once years ago. *Stay off Ellis.* An old story about a lumber accident, some curious wander crushed by a falling log. It's structure like a boogieman tale to scare children. Like all taboos it worked in reverse, giving him an obsessive interest in the unremarkable gravel road. It lay just a mile to the east bordering the giant Kindred farm, dark forrest at that end, soy and corn for acres on the other.

"Like I was saying, of a more mysterious nature."

Bullet looked up to see if he could still see JJ through the trees.

"What are you gettin' on about?" He asked Nelson.

"Sightings aren't as rare as you might think, Mr. Bullet. Colloquially it's called the Grassman, but, man, no, I don't think so. Multi-regionally it's called Bigfoot, and our Canadian brothers call it Sasquatch."

"You think the Grassman killed our dogs?"

"I can't say, Mr. Bullet. What I can say is that it's awfully peculiar."

Bullet looked at the sky. "Buzzards pick 'em clean this evening."

He leaned the umbrella against his shoulder, and Goat aimed his gun at Nelson and snapped the trigger. Nelson forced a concerned smile at the boy.

"Just not sure this is the right place for a boy his size."

Bullet looked down at the boy as if eyeing him for his size and weight. "My daddy didn't keep me from the butcher when I was a boy, and it's done right by me. 'Sides Goat's seen it all. Ain't ya boy?"

The boy shook his head and looked at Nelson.

"Children can be sensitive to blood and guts and things of a ...gory nature."

Mostly maple and oak there. Low lying forest that confused passage through the woods, vines and thorns growing up and hanging from the trees, a path choked in green. He could just make out their voices, Bullet's Appalachian drawl. He looked back. Could be an argument. Ahead, up along the forest ridge he thought he saw a man but shook his head and followed the deer path. A twig snapped and he looked up again at the tree, a shadow, bristled poison ivy vine, a tall figure stared, striking JJ shocked and frightened with his mouth open. He wondered how long it watched him in silence. It turned and ran, a hairy bear head bobbing and body hunched, shirking through the woods. He followed with the thorns at his pants. Tearing up through the underbrush and panting when he came to the ridge top. It was gone, only a shaking bush. He looked for tracks, calmed his breathing and listened but the rain was falling heavier now, loud in the leaves.

"Listen, you youth minister mother fucker, I'm not raising a pussy," said Bullet sticking his finger in the deputies face.

Nelson stunned into silence looked at the boy, Goat, then back at Bullet.

"Alrighty," said Nelson and put his eye back to the camera.

JJ walked out of the woods covered in cocklebur his shoulder smarting from brushing against a Hawthorn trunk.

"Whaddya find detective? Took ya long enough," said Bullet walking up to him. He jerked a thumb at Nelson in the distance stooped at his camera over one of the dogs. "Get him off my property before I strangle his ass."

JJ looked back up in the woods not quiet ready to talk yet. Nelson was folding up his tripod and working his way towards them through the rain.

"I believe that fool's just ate up with the dumb ass," said Bullet. "And I hear that's contagious."

"We'll go," JJ said.

Nelson snapped a photo of the two of them saying, "Smile."

He cranked the film in its roll. "Find anything?"

JJ opened his mouth and formed it to say a word looking off at the Kindred trailers, lost in a thought.

"Nope," he said.

October 1987

Amazing how fast it all goes. Ways of life what seemed impervious to change, been going on for hundreds and thousands of years, get dropped in less than a decade, with them young folks so stunned they don't know their ass from their hat. How the hell many species can we live without? The mammoth, the dodo, the saber tooth tiger, I guess the answer's alot. More'n ya might think, but the house of cards'll fall soon enough. If ya ever gone huntin' alone so deep in the woods that you can't hear the trains or see city lights no more or even hear the highway then you know just how quick you can slip back into hunger, survival, and that religious madness that comes out of the forest. As dark sets in something new takes over, and you can feel it in your bones. Insect ethics I call it, not a question in the world can't be remedied by it, those are behaviors without a single second guess. Try to squeeze one self conscious thought out of a dung beetle. Can't do it.

They thought all the black bears were gone in Ohio. Overhunted and driven out by settler's clear cutting. I didn't see one in the wild till I was twenty-nine. Scared the piss out of me, you know exactly what it is though, you see that honey colored muzzle. Makes ya feel good. Glad we ain't yet killed everything.

As the population comes back the box stores keep growing too ya know. They like restaurant dumpsters. (...)

2

He drove with the windows down, the sweat on his arms cool in the breeze, and an old rock tune playing. The evening sky was going red and the river was changing from brown to green. The trees kept low to the hills and overhung the roads that wound and dipped along the river. He passed over a creek bridge, his view always nose down, rarely able to see the birds-eye undulation of the hills and forest that grew dense and excessive. Down a dirt driveway the stars glowed between the trees, he bumped over a cattle gate.

A small woman in a thin cotton gown and a pile of curled gray hair stood on a farmhouse porch, her wrinkle-faced bloodhound at her feet and a rifle propped beside her on the deck rail. JJ got out of the truck. Before she spoke she pointed West beyond her barn; her hands covered in farm clay and shaking with arthritis.

"Heard'em over there, Forte."

JJ turned and looked out over a row of staked pole beans. "Out by the creek?"

Dragon flies dipped around her barn, hovered over the water in the housing of a huge tractor tire on its side.

"I was walking Milton and I heard something knocking around and bellowing some awful sound."

Her watery cataract eyes. Her mean stare. JJ put a hand on his hip. "That's what ya said last time, Mrs. Roman. And there weren't nothing out there."

"But this time I saw it. Milton, saw it too, didn't you?"

"Saw what?"

The cricket's whistling swelled and relaxed in the descending dusk.

"I don't know what it was," the woman said.

"How many times I been out here Mrs. Roman? April you said it was poachers. Now what?"

The woman just stared and listened.

"I hear it all the time."

JJ looked out with here. "Is it far, Mrs. Ro-?"

"Shh," she said sharply and inclined her ear to the woods.

JJ heard nothing.

"Just beyond those woods, just around the barn a piece. Mind the melons."

JJ checked his pistol and reholstered it. That frog croak that sounds like a dully struck wire.

"I'm sure it'll be fine, Mrs. Roman."

Behind the barn, JJ came to a barbed wire fence and pushed down the top with his hand and high-stepped over it. Ohio forest was low and thick with vine and it cracked underfoot and the sound carried in the dark. He came to a dried-out creek bed and walked in the dips made by the water. In the half-light shone the smooth rock. He paused to listen. Leaves shuffled to his left, he whipped his light onto a cedar tree and touched the butt of his pistol. The cedar was brown-orange and water-starved. Tiny thrush birds flew off startled.

A branch snapped, and he whipped the light back around. Limbs bent in the wind. He heard a voice, the hushed and hurried whisper of a gig-is-up human voice and he drew his gun. A honeysuckle bush shook and he put his finger near the trigger, and the bush continued to shake like something was stuck, and finally, he said, "What in God's name?"

A pig, no bigger than a house cat, waddled up to him snorting. It examined the sole of his boot, wagging its nearly hairless, white ass. "God damn," he said and lowered his gun. It nudged his boot with its wet snout and looked up at him excited, nearly beaming.

"Wait a minute..." he said, kneeling to look at the animal. "I know this pig." He looked up and called into the woods, "Stan?"

"James?" came a voice, closer than expected.

A tall, old man with a leather hat came out from behind a tree a few yards away carrying his own dim light and a wicker basket. "Well, I'll be, James, what are you doing here?"

"Dang it Stan, I almost shot your pig."

The good-natured animal went back to its owner squealing. "Not Cruella. Oh, dear." He bent over and scratched the pig's ears.

"You scared the piss out of me."

"What are you doing out here?"

"Stan, you're on Mrs. Roman's property. She's up at her house right now with a rifle in her lap."

"Oh my, oh dear. Have we come that far?"

"Yeah. God, come on, I'll drive y'all home."

"Oh, I appreciate it, James. Somehow we got turned around, and it got late on us, didn't it, Cruella? And my sense of direction isn't what it used to be. But, my God, look at what we've got, look at these." He tipped the wicker basket so JJ could see the brown, bread-colored heads of the mushrooms, big as a fist.

"You better hide those," JJ said.

Milton raised his tired head and gave out one deep bark as they approached and Mrs. Roman stood out of her rocking chair and pointed her rifle.

"Mrs. Roman! It's us. It's JJ."

"Jesse put your gun down, honey," Stan said.

"Stanley?"

"Hi."

"What are you doing in my woods, there are poachers out there."

"I think your poachers was these two, Mrs. Roman."

The pig was content to smell the Bronco's tires, first the front passenger side and then moving hurriedly to the back one.

"No," she said, "I saw him. A tall man. Taller than Stanley."

JJ looked at Stan. Stan was six feet.

"Ok, well, I'm gonna take Stan and the pig home, Mrs. Roman."

"What do you have there?" Mrs. Roman pointed at the basket.

Stan held a truffle up and turned his flashlight on it.

"Mushrooms."

"I don't suppose you found those on my land?"

"Well," he paused. "I can't be certain. We've been hunting since a little past four."

"Those are mine, Stanley."

JJ caught Stan's eye. He crawled in the driver's seat and gave the old man a told-ya-so shrug.

"I'll give you some, Jesse, you and Milton."

She looked a little closer at the mushroom and frowned and waved her hand in dismissal. "You old fool."

"Come on, Stan, let's get out of Mrs. Roman's way."

She stood her rifle against her shoulder and said, "They are still out there Sheriff."

"I'm not the Sheriff, Mrs. Roman."

"Oh, I know that. What are you gonna do? They are still out there."

"Bye Mrs. Roman, bye Milton."

Cruella stuck her head out the window and sniffed at the rushing wind. Stan held her with both hands.

"How ya doing, James. I haven't seen you, well, since the funeral."

"Yeah, I guess. Tell ya, I kinda had a crummy day, Stan."

Stan paused and smiled at JJ. "Look like yer uncle."

"Yeah? I know."

"And you sound like your father."

"Really?"

"Sound exactly like him."

"Stan, you know these woods better than just about anybody."

"That's true. Your father was maybe the only other that knew them better."

"You ever seen any bear attacks or wolves on a rampage kill a bunch of animals?"

Stanley pondered it for a moment and slipped his cupped hand over the pig's muzzle.

"Can't say I've seen that," he said. "Me and yer uncle Glen was out along the river one evening hunting buck, and we came up on a herd of deer standing in a circle out in the field below. The sun was about to set and their shadows were stretched out and they stood pawing at the dirt for a minute and neither of us even moved to shoot. We looked at each other and then watched 'em. Had to be about ten of 'em. And then, like they had the thing choreographed, they took off in different directions, all at once. At camp that night, I asked Glen why he didn't shoot and he said, 'I just couldn't stop the council meeting.' That was it, a little glimpse."

JJ looked at him. He held the pig in his lap, and she sniffed him and he kissed her on the whiskery snout.

3

He pulled up the safety stick and slid his back door open to poke his head out. The hawk stood watching from the makeshift lean-to rigged up to the trailer wall. Her marble eyes glared; her movements saccadic and abrupt. She preened, expressionless and intense. He slid the door open the rest of the way and whispered, "That's a good girl. That's a good girl." She bent to examine the leash wire attached to her foot.

"How's that wing, Percy?"

The bird scuttled back and forth on its perch, nervously preening her down feathers, her muscles twitching.

The washed-out grey sky was heavy with rain. In the trailer, the refrigerator light cast his sharp shadow on the wall. He shook an empty milk container and sighed at the barren landscape of condiments and leftovers and unwrapped the butcher paper on a small package.

He placed a square of squirrel meat on the deck rail and backed away. She opened her white wings and lifted herself into the air and grabbed the meat, tearing at it with her beak. One alien eye kept on JJ, making small clicking sounds with her talons and beak as she ate and hopped on the rail. He opened a lawn chair and sat and watched her; a beer bottle beading with perspiration in his hand. The trees whished and rattled out beyond his overgrown yard. Lightning bugs flashed in the grass. One flared in front of JJ, and he reached out and it landed on his index finger, where slowly it circled, glowing. A bat flew, its wings skittering like a stop motion film.

He woke, crick-necked, to raindrops plodding on the deck. Percy eyed him from her house, and he asked how she was doing and if she ever slept. She squawked.

"I'm going, I'm going," he said, folding up the chair. He knocked over the empty beer bottle, and it rolled along the deck roaring until it slipped between two rails and fell silent into the grass. In the slapping rain, he came down the steps into his yard, the grass at his shins. He got on his knees and ran his hands around to feel for the bottle. It was nowhere. The earth swallows whole, without end. Thunder wrecked the soft night and the rain stopped. JJ went inside and dried himself. He threw his clothes on the couch and went to bed naked.

Laying wide-eyed with damp hair, he dreamt clouds like cotton candy spinning above the world as Buck Owens sang about them. His friends from high school on the lake driving cars fast across the calm waters laughing and smiling, optimistic and young. Kathy's hyena laugh over the rumbling of the Nova. Colleen, Ricky, Weasel, and JJ himself skiing on the rope and jumping in the wake of Darrell's Chevy truck.

A week later JJ was out with the mower. He cut two strips along the deck when the bottle exploded rattling like stones in the blades. He cut the engine and raised the front wheels. Mixed in the grass the bottle shined like slivers of crystal, elemental and baroque. A bee crawled out of the weeds and flew away. He left the mower and went back inside.

October 1987

This was '70, '71 maybe. Ole boy up near Columbus had too much money and no sense to go with it. Had a massive collection of exotic animals: lions, kangaroos, bears, snakes, you name it, he had one. One night he gets amped up on LSD and lets them all go. Fella went crazy. Naked except for a pair of flip-flops when the cops came in with their lights. And next thing ya know there's kangaroos in playgrounds. The news told people not to run if they encountered something. They'd chase ya down. Nobody got hurt, that I know of. And me, I got called up kinda late in the game. First thing I saw when I got there was a monkey sitting Buddha calm in the back of a police cruiser, watching the mystery unfold. The sheriff, dapper fella, forget his name, was talking to the news stations like a celebrity. A tiger got hit by a semi-truck in Fernvale and the news left out of there to go see if they could get a picture. Wasn't anything left of the tiger. And that poor truck driver. Channel 5 showed him standing in the rain at the foot of the truck shaking his head in shock. Musta felt he was dreaming a tiger. Musta felt a heavy remorse when he reckoned he wasn't.

They closed the schools and advised everyone to stay in. You imagine a kid seeing a tiger on the walk to school? It all limber and hunched low on a jungle gym. Why it could swallow a child whole. I rode in the back of a pickup with a bunch of local police driving through the suburbs. People stood at their windows watching us go by. I told them a wild animal won't hang around with all their trucks rumbling up and down the streets. We spent all night driving and searching for wild game, like a bizarre, suburban safari.

By the next morning, they were missing just two things on their list. A gibbon monkey, which they never did find far as I remember, and a male lion. Showed us a picture of the playboy with his arms around its neck. I didn't see how it could hide for very long in the sprawl. I felt sorry for him, cause I didn't think he'd live through it.

Sure enough, it was spotted that day casually sauntering through someone's backyard. We took three trucks, two officers in each, and wheeled up into a nice neighborhood. There were hundred thousand dollar homes and not a soul around. You might imagine, we found it pretty quick. Stretched out on his belly up in the shade of a back porch munching on a poodle. I shit ya not. One of those little fluffy white ones. We watched it from the neighbor's yard two doors down with binoculars just gawking in disbelief. You could hear its teeth crushing the bones. Eventually, it took notice of us and stood to go, still carrying lunch in its mouth. A deputy shot it in the head from 100 yards. Heck of a shot. It fell in the grass, and we watched his chest heaving up and down. I bagged it. From a distance, it was beautiful. Its mane sleek and muscles lean and strong but up close you could tell it was malnourished, mangy, the ribs a little too prominent.

He must have been confused from the get-go. Taming a wild animal fudges its boundaries. The very idea is ignorant. For a man to keep a creature like that caged for his own, it's a sin. And I suppose that was its owner's revelation as well when he had this drug-induced spiritual epiphany or whatever. 'Course I have no sympathy for the man, even though I heard he wept for the cat and have little doubt he loved it. It's the problem with sins of this nature, they bleed outside the confines of your own soul. If one spent an afternoon he could perhaps trace the various players, the various actors, and thinkers that must bear a portion of the responsibility for the death of this lion and the poodle. The work would prove unending, and this diagram of guilt would include the father's father and so on, on down. No small task. All the same, a thin skin divides us. Is he solely responsible? No. But I hope he carried crushing guilt all the same. He did some time for animal abuse, paid some fines, but the last thing I heard when he got out a few years later, he sued the state for killing the lion, and he lost.

4

When JJ came into the office the next morning, rifling through the mail, Donna was wet. The front of her dress dark with water and she looked at JJ with a startled, mute alertness that worried him. The fan was oscillating, flapping the American flag that stood on a pole in a wooden wine barrel with their umbrellas, and then turning to Donna whipping at the corner of her dress. She held an 8 by 10 photograph of JJ as a boy kneeling in a baseball uniform smiling with buck teeth at the camera and this was also glistening wet. There were wet photos arranged on the floor around her desk and trailing back to his office where the door stood open. A photo from Halloween 1972 of JJ dressed as Zorro, a picture of his mother as a young lady. Donna watched him. He poked his head in his office and there was a hole in the ceiling where the tiles had broken and his desk was moved and there was a puddle of water on the floor.

Donna said, "I came and fed the animals and watered the plants and took out the trash and when I sat down at my desk I heard this tapping. Tap. Tap. Tap. And I thought, that's coming from the office, and so I peeked in," Donna was talking with her hands while she walked over to JJ at his office door. "Just peeked, and turned on the lights, but I couldn't figure out where it was coming from, so I went around your desk and then I looked up and there it was, this bulge in the ceiling tiles and I knew if that thing broke it would soak your nice desk."

JJ was looking at the gaping hole in the ceiling and at the water on the floor and at a series of new unopened boxes.

"And so I pushed the desk out of the way and I thought I would just poke the ceiling, you know, and catch all the rainwater before you had to come in and deal with all this and see your whole office in disarray."

His father's purple heart sat on the floor in the office drying and he picked it up.

"I needed something to stand on so I could prod it and catch the water in the trashcan and so I pushed over one of your filing cabinets and stood on it and poked it and it just came down like a flood. I mean soaked everything. But there it was, a whole 'nother stash of boxes and files up in the ceiling that your father had stashed up there."

He lifted a flap on one of the boxes. A few matchbox cars, a letter opener he had used as a play knife, his father's wedding ring, a book on tracking animals, an old spyglass, his father's diploma from the police academy, and a picture of he and his father in Conservator's uniform when he had first been hired. 8 track tapes and more envelopes full of pictures. He shuffled through the tapes: Nashville Gold. Kenny Rogers. Dolly. Hank Williams, 38 Special. Allman Brothers. And one with a label written in his father's blocky script: OCTOBER 1987. It was also signed: James Joseph Forte, Sr.

JJ looked up suddenly at Donna and came around his desk and looked for the key behind the filing cabinet, but it was gone.

"When I was getting down I found it."

Donna held the key out for JJ to see.

"I knew right away what it went to."

"Jesus. Listen, Donna..."

"What's the money from, JJ?"

"You went through my desk?"

"I'm sorry, JJ."

"I can't believe you just went through my shit, Donna."

"What's the money from, JJ?"

"Nothing."

"Nothing?" She sat down at her desk.

"It's nothing."

"JJ, you gotta tell me."

JJ looked at the drawer in the desk and pulled at it.

"I locked it back," Donna said.

He walked to the foot of the office and leaned an elbow against the door jamb and hung his head. She looked at him.

"Something Dad set up, some logging thing. He told me somebody died in a logging accident a long time ago and that's it. There's some people just didn't want any more accidents. That's all it is, Donna. I swear. That's all I know."

"It's Kindred money."

"Donna," JJ looked up and came to her desk. "The less ya know the better."

She put the key in her pocket. "I want fifty percent."

"What? That's ridiculous."

"Is it?"

"Jesus, Donna, you and my father were friends."

"Honey, I knew your dad as good as anybody, but I didn't know he was accepting bribe money."

He looked down at the pendant with the profile of George Washington in his hand.

"I'm raising two teenage boys, JJ. One of which I found smoking pot in my basement last week."

"Finn?"

"Thomas."

"I'm sorry, Donna."

"I'd like them both to go to college."

"Can I have my key back?"

"Fifty percent."

"Thirty."

The front door swung open and Nelson waltzed in with a box of donuts. He said, "Hi y'all," whistling the tune from MASH.

Donna gave JJ one more long look and said, "Morning Nelson."

"What's going on?"

"Donna found some new boxes."

"Is this you, JJ?"

"Yeah, Halloween, I was Zorro."

"Freaking fantastic. Donut Donna?" he asked and held the box open for her.

"I think I will, Nelson."

"I already ate the apple ones."

"I'll take a Maple glazed, thank you."

"You're soaked. What the heck is going on this morning anyhow?"

Nelson followed the photographs into JJ's open office door and said, "Well, the roof's leaking, that's the problem. Dang right down on your desk, huh?"

"Thirty," said JJ to Donna. "Yep, right above the desk."

"Gotta story for ya, bossman," said Nelson, then he paused and said, "Has anyone fed Rascal? Watch this."

Nelson crammed one entire glazed donut into his mouth and smiled at JJ with the dough ballooning between his teeth and JJ shaking his head.

"Nelson, you're a wonder."

"Fank you mossman," he said.

"Nelson, you might have called my dad boss, but not me."

"Nah, he didn't like it either," said Nelson, swallowing. "So there is this lady, one Ms. Brown; I knew Ms. Brown's niece when I was a teacher down in Tennessee, and we hit it off. So I get a call from Ms. Brown because Sherry, the niece, told her who I was, right? Feel like I know her already. And she's not a crazy person like some of the others, JJ. This one is for real. Lives on a apple orchard right off Bifork up near the lake."

Nelson dropped the donuts on his desk and holstered his gun.

"I knew Sherry when I was a teacher down in Knoxville. She studied fashion at the university there and made clothes you'd never wear on the street. I don't know where you'd wear this stuff. Like a dress completely clear except for the thread in the seams, you ever seen that? I mean you could see everything, nipples, and everything."

"Nelson, how much coffee you had this morning?"

"Couple cups."

JJ nodded.

"What?"

JJ and Donna smirked and looked at each other.

"You better go with him," Donna said. "Or there'll be another piece in the paper about a lizard boy living in a creek."

"That newspaper man misquoted me."

JJ closed his office and put his rain slicker on and followed Nelson to the door but paused. "Donna, can you call about fixing the roof while we're gone?"

"Sure, JJ."

"And maybe get out of those wet clothes, huh?"

"K, boss."

5

The warm, fatty smell of the fast-food filled the Bronco, and as they drove through the town square with its rusted cannons and bronze monuments, they feast.

"Nelson, here's the thing," JJ said between french fries. "You believe in so much that ya lose your credibility." JJ extended a finger for each thing on the list. "You believe in aliens. You believe in bigfoot. You believe in ghosts. You probably believe in angels and demons and chakras and the Mothman."

"Now hold on, JJ, I tell ya, I saw it." Nelson sucked from his big gulp.

They passed an abandoned wooden shack with a caved-in roof and its windows busted.

"I tell ya, I saw it. A spirit. Or a soul. Or something. We saw it."

Nelson stuffed his mouth with burger.

"Where's your proof bud, huh?"

" Nelson chewed and swallowed and said, "This was real."

"Alright. So what did it look like?"

"It was glowing."

"Glowing?"

"Yeah."

"Like in the movies?"

"It's hard to describe, JJ. It was like seeing something in the corner of yer eye, but only while you looked straight at it. And he had on old clothes."

"Old clothes?"

"Civil War old."

They pulled up to a stoplight and waved to an old man sitting at a bus stop. Behind him stood what was left of the library that burned years before, its charcoal interior exposed to the sun.

"You're messing with me?"

"I swear it. Scared your dad pale."

"My dad saw it?"

"We were together."

"Oh," said JJ. "My dad didn't suffer fools."

"No, he didn't."

"What did he say about it?"

"He said he thought we hallucinated from a gas leak."

"That's my dad. Maybe he was right?"

"I didn't smell any gas. Right up there. It was right up there."

JJ put his blinker on and pulled into the turn lane and they looked down a narrow railway tunnel, only big enough for one car at a time.

"Nelson, if I saw a ghost, I mean if I really saw one, I'd go back there every night and wait."

"That's a good point. I never did go back," Nelson said, "but you can bet your butt your dad did."

"You're messing with me."

"I swear it. It was right down there," Nelson pointed to the other end of the tunnel. "A teenage boy standing right there with one of those Union hats on his head."

The train tracks ran across the top on heavy squared timber logs and coal-black gravel. It was cool inside and a road sign cast a soft square of light on the rough rounded concrete wall. Neither spoke as they drove through.

"I didn't see anything did you, Nelson?"

"Ha. ha."

"Ya know what, the truly alarming thing is that they don't exist. No angels, no demons, no ghosts. Nothing's out there. Now that's fucking terrifying." JJ ate another chicken nugget.

Nelson reached the end of his pop and slurped at the last drop searching around with his straw. "That's the saddest thing I've ever heard you say. Don't you believe in a soul?"

"A soul? Sure, I don't know. Maybe. Yeah, I believe in James Brown, the king of soul."

JJ pulled the Bronco over at the front of a two-story gothic house with a big porch supported by wooden columns and a wrought iron fence.

"Well, I believe in King James and the gospels."

"Yeah? How's that working out?"

A well-dressed man and his young wife and son stood on the porch waiting, the woman had her face buried in her husband's shoulder. They got out of the truck and Nelson said, "I'd say God's been treating me pretty good."

JJ unhooked the fence and called, "Ya'll the Shavers, I reckon?"

The man stepped forward and put his hands on his son's shoulders and waved JJ and Nelson up to the porch.

"I'm Jerry Shaver." The woman took her head out of the man's arm and her eyes were bright red from crying. The boy would not look up at JJ or Nelson.

"JJ Forte. This is Nelson Turner."

"Howdy do?"

"This is my wife, Sandra, and my son, Charlie. Charlie's the one that found it."

JJ bent down to eye level with the boy. "What did ya see, son?"

"My cat."

"Yeah?"

"I'll take you back there. Yer other man is already here. He arrived just before yall."

JJ and Nelson exchanged a glance. "I'm sorry what?" JJ said.

Mr. Shaver, loosening his silk tie, led JJ and Nelson around the porch to the back yard where a heavy-set young man in the gray Animal Control collared shirt and black pants stood at the edge of the fence. He stared down at a black tomcat, dead and laid out on its side. The man looked up when he saw them coming and shook his head.

"Winston?"

"Well, if it ain't Forte, the all-mighty Game Warden."

"He's not with you?" asked the father.

"Winston," said Nelson in greeting.

"Nelson. No, we ain't together," said the doughy man to Mr. Shaver. "Late as usual. This is my crime scene so you boys can just go on."

"What's going on?," said Mr. Shaver.

"You can't have a crime scene, Winston," JJ said. "Winston is Animal Control. We are with Fish and Wildlife."

Winston stood a few steps between the cat and the Fish and Wildlife men and they circled around him, JJ veering right and Nelson left, and then Winston began to circle, they watching each other the whole time and the dead cat in the middle looking rigidly pale and very dead. Mr. Shaver stood with his hand on his hips watching in confusion.

"Why don't yall go back to fish and wildlifing, this is domestic."

"Winston, we're here, so we're gonna take a look."

"Sir, we really don't need them; I'm worried they will contaminate the site."

"Winston shut the hell up. I'm sorry," JJ said to Mr. Shaver.

"Listen, I don't really want to be part of any fighting. My family is worried about our cat."

"It's under control, sir," said JJ.

"Yeah, animal control," Winston said.

"Nelson, could you gag this idiot?"

"So what's the story, Winston?" Nelson asked.

Winston turned his head and said, "Clearly, we've got a murdered cat."

The father held his hand to his mouth.

"Murdered?" said JJ.

"You scoff? I'd say she was killed less than six hours ago."

"He," said Mr. Shaver.

"And why do you think that, Sherlock?" asked Nelson.

"Dew's wet under the cat."

Nelson bent down. Mouth slightly open, green eyes wide, fanged teeth exposed, the cat looked like a Halloween puppet. The skin was removed in an oval shape revealing the muscles of the chest and genitals. "Weird," said Nelson and then turned to the man and said, "No offense."

"It's very disturbing," said the man. "You think it was murdered?"

"Probably a satanic ritual of some sort," said Winston

"Oh my God."

"Sir, don't listen to him," said JJ. "We don't know what this is."

"JJ, the genitals are gone."

The paws, both front and back, were crossed over each other and there was no blood. Nelson put on a pair of latex gloves and turned on his flashlight.

"Ya'll ain't touched it at all?" JJ asked the man.

"No, no. We didn't touch it, him, his name is Black Cat," the man said.

"Creative." JJ put a piece of gum in his mouth.

Nelson lifted the hind legs of the cat with a pen and laid it back down. "Did he have a tail?"

"Yes," said the man.

With the pen tip, Nelson pulled back the stiff lips and examined the teeth.

"Was he missing?" asked JJ.

"No, I fed him last night. About dark. He came up purring like he always does."

"Why don't you guys leave this up to me. I mean, I'm Animal Control, not you guys."

JJ put a finger to his lips and said, "Shhh."

"Holy cow," said Nelson.

"What is it?" asked the man.

"Stitches."

"Stitches?" said Winston.

Nelson snapped some close-ups then took a pair of small scissors from his belt and carefully cut the sutures.

"Holy cow," said Nelson.

"What?" said the man.

"Could ya ease up on the Holy cows, Nelson?"

"They took out its organs. Its heart. The heart is gone. And there's no blood at all..."

"Oh my God."

Nelson reached in the cat's chest and tugged at something and the cat seemed grotesquely animated with the head nodding as he pulled. He brought out a bird skull.

"I'm gonna throw up," said Mr. Shaver.

"What is it?" asked Winston.

"I'd say this was a pigeon."

"Dove," said JJ.

"Yeah, maybe a dove."

"My God," said Mr. Shaver. He turned to JJ and said, "Could he have eaten a bird?"

"No sir," Nelson said and stood and shined his light on the skull, "that's where the heart should be. It's been drained of blood"

JJ scratched his hair.

"Satanic ritual," said Winston shaking his head.

"What the hell am I supposed to tell my family?"

"What do you think, JJ?" asked Nelson.

JJ looked at the man and at the cat and paused. "I think the world's full of fucked up people. Pardon my French, sir."

"What do you think it means?" asked Mr. Shaver. "I mean, we've gotta find the people that did this."

Nelson said, "Do you or your family have any enemies you're aware of?"

"Enemies? My God. No, I don't have any enemies. I work at the bank."

"Are you a religious man, Mr. Shaver?" Nelson took him gently by the arm and led him away from the cat.

JJ looked at Winston and said, "So you don't know anything about this?"

"I know as much as y'all."

"You didn't do it, did ya, Winston?"

JJ studied Winston's eyes. Winston looked at him to see if he was kidding.

"You guys are so mean to me. No, I didn't do it."

"We are Winston. We are. But ya ain't good at your job. Part of your job is to gather roadkill. And who ends up hauling all your dead possums and all the dead skunks to the trash? Me and Nelson. Well, I'm not covering your ass anymore. You wanna start a new life as a responsible Animal Control employee? You can begin by bagging this mutilated kitty."

"You're a dick, Forte."

"Yeah? Maybe."

Nelson led Mr. Shaver back to the cat saying, "I'd recommend holy water for at least a week in the mornings and go on and get ya a rosary, do some hail mary's, it ain't gonna hurt ya. In a week's time, you could have the devil fully exorcised from this yard. Good as new. What do you think, JJ?"

"I think Winston is gonna take care of the body for us."

"Oh great." Nelson put the bird skull in Mr. Shaver's hand and the man looked down at it.

They left Winston fussing the cat into a trash bag.

Back in the truck, JJ sighed. They sat quiet for a long minute until the CB buzzed and they both spooked a little.

Nelson took his drink from the cup holder and slurped up the ice that had melted. He wiggled the straw in the paper cup and sat it back.

"JJ, there is more things in heaven and earth than are dreamt of in your philosophy," Nelson said.

"Nelson," said JJ. "You know that's Shakespeare, not Bible."

"Oh, oh yeah."

6

He sat on the porch with his boots covered in the tall grass. A mosquito settled on his arm in its delicate way. He swatted it flat leaving a blood-smeared stain on his arm. His parents' Buick, layered in grime and pollen, sat dormant in the drive. Purple blooming ground ivy decorated the yard.

The master bedroom was crowded with milk crates full of books, books by trappers and falconers, and boxes full of his mother's dresses, dresses from the sixties with white leather belts, and cheap green jewelry. The room smelled of trapped air, and the carpets felt full of sand. On the floor were yellowed New York Times, Wildlife magazines, National Geographic, safety manuals on gun care, How To Bandage Wounds In The Wild, collections of tin cans and glass bottles. The old man must have saved every coke bottle he ever drank. Each wrapped in newsprint for a truncated purpose.

He moved a few crates to get to the closet. A sleeping bag fell from its high wedge and rolled open on the floor where a wolf spider as big as a child's shoe ran under the bed. Corduroy coats, and overalls, button-down shirts, new neckties with their store tags. He stood on a suitcase to reach the highest shelf and found covered in dust the rectangular faux wood-paneled 8 track player.

He cleared a place on the table in the living room between the salt shakers and the three large lawn jockey sculptures and examined the silver-plated face with its worn plastic buttons and the rubber wire in the back.

On his hands and knees, he found an outlet under the oak dresser that housed his mother's china and plugged in the 8 track, and sat on the springy velvet couch. He put the one labeled *OCTOBER 1987* into the deck and pushed the play button.

"Okay, Okay. Test one, two," came his father's sand-raked voice. There was a long pause and a shifting like fabric brushing across the microphone, then a click and his father's deep drawl, *"I mean they come out of nowhere. Great* dizzy *clouds of em. All of Irontown was infested with these quarter-sized gypsy moths."*

JJ stopped the tape. A serious voice; he could, based on the way he pronounced *nowhere,* tell that his father had been drinking. JJ ran his hands over his face. "What are you up to, old man? I need a drink."

He clicked it on and upped the volume. *"Hit so many with the truck I could scoop'em off the windshield in handfuls. They was something awful in the trees. Hundreds of old oaks died. For weeks it was hell."* In the kitchen, he poured a shot of bourbon and listened to his father's heavy hunter's protraction. The voice distant and muffled but familiar. He capped the whisky and put it back on the high shelf, but stopped and took it down again and poured another drink and sat it next to the speaker.

"For you, pops."

He woke on the couch. A Michigan-shaped drool stain on the pair of pants he used as a pillow. His father was still going. *"People die in car wrecks every day on the 52 headed to Cincy."* He stopped the tape and looked up at the clock. It wasn't yet midnight.

Light-headed, sparks moving at the edge of his vision, he stumbled to the hallway and stubbed a toe on a chair leg. He hobbled to the bathroom and felt along the smooth texture of the floral wallpaper for the light switch. Blinded, he leaned a hand against the wall to steady himself and looked at his reflection as he pissed. He looked like Uncle Glen, stoop-shouldered like him. When he was twelve he went on a fishing trip to Kyler Creek with Glen. He remembers his smallness as he tried to reel a fish. Glen would stretch the line into the water with ease like he knew where to put it. The cold water in the canoe soaked his socks in his shoes and the shadeless sun was hard and ruthless. He stared at his own mean eyes and brushed his teeth. When he lay back down he said if he was his dead uncle what news was that?

In his dream, a slow-moving fog, chemical pink, floated above dead grass. With his heavy limbs he lumbered into it, arms outstretched. He watched the lightning bugs gather on the window above the foyer door. Tomato red stripes on their wings, flashing their green, signals in synchronized patterns, a hypnotic Morse code of bioelectrically moving messages.

Awake, Awake, oh sleeper, but beware, horde not treasures on earth where moths and rust doth corrupt.

In his father's study, lengthy bookshelves lined the walls, and the massive shield and crossed swords of the family crest was mounted above a rolltop desk where he found gun and horse magazines, letters, birthday cards, a pair of his grandmother's tiny gloves, a freshwater pearl, a rusted Bowie knife. His mother was outside. He called to her, went to the window, and yelled her name. She turned and waved. She was young. The woman before his birth he knew only from photos. Perhaps she did not recognize him because she kept walking and disappeared behind a brick wall.

The pink fog rose out of the carpet into the dark and vaulted room. A drawer in the top of the desk opened and papers poured out. The roll-top shunted open and another drawer slid out coughing out more paper, and another, a cascade of junk mail and bills and photographs and letters. Like a cartoon cat trying to plug holes in a cracking dam, JJ tried to shut the drawers.

Then there was a cartoon cat. A cat in overalls one finger at a time plugging the cyan fountains spouting balletically from breaking seams. Medical records and dollar bills. Soon the room was full of water and wet paper and they began to swirl and drain. The cat screamed and was sucked underneath. Words fell out of their places and swam into eddies of illegible froth. The currency clung wet and heavy to JJ's legs and chest, and the water reached his waist. He grabbed a handrail and pulled himself onto a narrow staircase rising out of the basement. His body was slug-heavy, arms of brick and legs of concrete. At the top stood a mud-drenched bear, rearing up on its hind legs suddenly haloed by the strobing insect light on the window. It roared and the house shook. Slobber rained in loops from its purple gums and the pink tongue vibrated so fast it blurred. Then the bear inhaled and JJ felt himself carried up by the breath into the terrible mouth. He slid a hand into the warm wet sulcus where the dark gum wrapped tooth and held for life, his feet dropping into the fractal throat. Waters rose out of the beasts' belly up to JJ's chest, then his neck, then his chin, and at last his eyelashes batted at the waterline. The drowned cartoon cat bobbed face down in the water beside him. He entered the stream, floating under the paper sea littered with his parent's stuff, the kitchen table cantilevering one leg above in open air, the maroon Buick gushing bubbles in a corpuscular froth as it sank out of sight, the bed, mattress and all floating on the surface, an easy chair descending and turning in the algid syrup and finally touching the ground in a thump disturbing a cloud of bottom muck and scattering the button-eyed deep-sea catfish with feathered leer growing out of their corpulent heads swimming in water so black he lost himself and dove down, down to a grave full of aciculated bones adorned in the scrimshaw designs of Viking ships, thin and piercing, and down and down he went.

ACT TWO

1

Young saplings grew in the gravel road leading back to the abandoned strip mine. They hit the Broncos fender. The leaves shook and the boughs bent and tucked under scrapping the truck chassis and then came springing back in the wake bent. The tall grass, still wet with dew, left streaks on the doors and the headlight's gray beams lit the morning fog. He came out into a flat plain of dark gravel and dried mud where almost nothing grew. The mine descended in rings each half a football field in width and each covered in a darker, deader ash.

He stopped the Bronco and climbed out. Mercurial dust spun in his footfalls leaving grooved replicas of his boots. A children's moon hung in the open sky, and the sun was rising just above the far treeline, furnace red. It was so low on the horizon he could look right at it. The sheer enormity of the empty mine stunned him into a sullen silence. It was as if walking at the edge of hell where almost nothing lived, only the scrub grass and leafless shrubs surrounded by mountains of soot-colored gravel.

He kicked at a dried thistle bush and it bounced into the ash leaving chicken scratch like a child's illegible script. He climbed down one of the dusty switchbacks. A bird trilled far away. He looked for it across the waste. A backhoe's disembodied arm stood elbow up, the scoop full of giant galvanized nails. Below the excavated ditch was full of semi-transparent brown water, submerged refrigerators and tires, and other appliances illegally dumped, visible below the surface. Orange and blue chemical skims pooled at the water's edge.

Along the edge of the ashen surface, skeletal trees stood dusted in the white and grey of the eroded earth. JJ touched one of the knobby branches and it broke like charcoal in his fingers. Further on the forest grew dense and lush, overtaken with kudzu. He walked over rows of grooved tire marks and came to a white rock the size of a football sitting in the dust. He picked it up and was surprised at how light it was. He thumbed the dust off the bottom and looked at the slatted and delicate undercarriage of an animal skull. He pondered it and traced the eye socket to its jagged nostril hole and the black teeth. It was a bear skull with its prominent canines, and groupings of back premolars, set off by the powerful jaw from the front incisors. Then he found a jawless possum skull. Using a piece of rebar lying there he worked free a leg bone.

Nelson showed up in the other truck. He climbed out smiling and waved at JJ then snapped his fingers and went back in the truck and come out with two cups of coffee.

"What's up? Coffee for you. And I brought the camera."

"Good."

Nelson stretched his back and looked around. "L&L sure ain't planted no trees."

"Ner a one. See that ridge? There's bones just down there."

"What kind of bones?"

"All kinds, it's some kind of mass animal grave."

"Mother Mary."

JJ sipped the coffee.

"Lordy," said Nelson. "It's dry as the moon up here."

A repetitive knocking rose from the trees out behind them. Nelson's eyes opened wide and he smiled. "Oh man, hear that woodpecker. I ain't seen one in ages. He's big by the sound of him."

JJ led Nelson through the dust. Two small hunters in a desert crisscrossed by the beveled tracks of heavy machinery. JJ showed him all he had found and kneeled in the fly ash and pulled out another bone, white and pristine. He placed it in the long row of skulls he had excavated.

"Holy cow. It's like a..."

"Yeah," JJ said.

"Deer," said Nelson walking slowly down the line. "Is that a dog?"

"Look a little closer."

"Damn, JJ. That's a bear."

"Yeah."

Nelson snapped a photo and lowered the camera and was about to say something but closed his mouth and went on taking pictures, moving JJ around like a film director.

"Hold that in the light, there. Turn it left a little."

He moved JJ's hands so that the shadow fell across the eye sockets.

"Okay, get that one there, what is that, a possum?"

"I ain't sure we need to catalog every damn one, Nelson."

JJ walked off into the ash and Nelson snapped a picture of him squatting in the dust. He stood and slowly came back toward Nelson. Nelson yawned. JJ sat on a tire.

"So whaddya think?" asked Nelson.

"Somebody hid 'em. A lot of them."

"Why?"

"You tell me," said JJ.

"I don't know."

"It's mostly roadkill it looks like, based on the crushed skulls and snapped bones. Not many bullet holes. But we got a bear and a coyote in there. Protected animals."

"Was it L&L?"

JJ just looked out at the spiraling tracks on the ground.

"I don't know. I don't get it." Nelson said. "It's a real head-scratcher."

JJ got up and poked at something shining in the ash and pulled out a brown glass bottle, wiped it off. There a cowboy etched in glass rode a bucking horse. "Ah shit," JJ said.

"What's that?"

JJ held it to the light. "Dad's brand."

"Oh."

A little bit of liquid swished inside and a cigarette butt swam there; he tipped it and spilled the contents. "Oh," said Nelson again in a higher pitch. JJ tossed it end over end out into the dust. A small cloud rose and was stolen by the wind.

JJ turned to the bones and put his hands on his hips. He looked at Nelson.

"Well, it ain't hurting nobody, I guess," he said.

"No, it ain't. You want me to-" An airplane roared across the sky above them leaving two white streams as it went, and Nelson put his hands to his eyes and watched it and waited for the sound to die down. "You want me to develop these pictures?"

"Nah, sure, hell, I don't know. Ain't like we can fine him."

Nelson pulled the lap out of the back of the camera and exposed the film.

"There. Don't worry about it."

"Don't plan on it. I hate paperwork as much as the old man did."

December 1987

Them mountain roads wind up 'round Hanging Rock like spiderwebs. Most so gully washed you need a four-wheel drive. And you get up in there real deep, all the way back in there and sometimes you can find the spiders. Those forgotten mountain folk that got no taste for towns and cities. It's like going back in time really. Twenty. Hell, thirty years. Men and women so weathered they look bark skinned. Words so muddled, you can barely understand what they say. Like they speaking they own language. Leftover from God know where and when. Well, I bridge these worlds, the poison of towns and the country's old-timers. I speak between them and reason with them about the cities. I apply town laws to those still committed to the old life. You head into a city, a big city, and it's like you found the future... But sometimes I ask myself why? What happens in the deep ain't no difference to most of us. So a buck gets killt out of season. People die in car wrecks every day on the 52 headed to Cincy, and somewhere a man kills himself every few minutes. I'm in all this red tape and I wonder, what have I become? A spokesman for progress? My guess is that a city's pollution is proportional to its cultural attractions. Well, if a tree falls in the forest and all that. It's got to the point where I throw my hands and say let them fall. Time will clean it all up. Right?

2

The skunk carcass came up off the hot asphalt like a pancake. The guts stuck, and JJ shimmied the flat shovel back and forth. It made a taffy sound peeling off the black tarmac and stunk a bitter chemical stench. Nelson grimaced and leaned against the truck watching. It came off the concrete a furred weightless husk that would not hold together. JJ shrugged and tossed what was left into the summer ditch overgrown in pokeberry weed the bent racemes heavy with the black fruit.

"Not much left of it."

"Nope, but you sure stirred up the stink."

JJ popped the trunk and made to put the shovel in but Nelson stopped him.

"Here," Nelson said and unleafed a black plastic bag and spread it over the shovel, and tied it off.

JJ slipped it in and closed the trunk making his paper coffee cup on the hood jiggling and Nelson reached over to steady it before it could tip and spill in the road.

JJ bent and gulped for clean air. It was 7:20 in the morning, and he was already sweating hard.

"It'll never smell right in there again," Nelson said.

"Lord, no it won't."

JJ took his coffee and headed back for the driver seat pausing for a van to pass. It pushed him back against the truck in a gust of hot air, nearly knocking the coffee from his left hand, but he pivot, raised his hand, and in a careful adjustment of the wrist kept all of the pitching coffee in the cup.

"Ha," he said, "See that, Nelson?"

Nelson opened the passenger door. "Lord's smiling today."

"Touche," said JJ.

"So you know where the Church of God's Hands is at?" Nelson asked.

"Is that the one over by the post office?" JJ asked Nelson climbing in the driver seat.

"No that's the United Methodist," said Nelson. "Church of God's Hands is the one on 5th street over by that bakery. What's the name of that bakery?"

"The one on 5th Street is the Primitive Baptists. Church of God's Hand is that big one off Main. Are you talking about Devin's Bagel Den?"

"Isn't the Primitive Baptists the one out beyond whatsit, over where Pam lives, off Lippitt?"

"Yeah, yeah, I think you're right," said JJ.

"Yeah, that's it, Devin's Bagel Den. Always thought it said Devil's Bagel Den."

"I think that one on 5th Street is First Pres."

Nelson latched his seat belt.

"Now wait. I think you're right. Church of God's Hands is that big one that's doing all that renovation."

JJ looked out at the sun beating down the morning's low summer steam that was rising up off the road. He turned the keys and popped the truck into gear and eased out onto the highway. They hit a bump where the road had been patched with a darker asphalt and his coffee lurched and spilled through the plastic rim hole all over his hand.

"Goddamnit," JJ said.

Nelson looked over at him.

3

The Reverend opened the side door. He wore a blue suit and tie and his dyed jet black hair was slicked back on his balding head. Three massive jeweled rings stood out on his fat hands.

"Come on in out of this rain, fellas," he said waving them inside.

They stamped their feet on a welcome rug. The Church of God's Hands felt cool and drafty inside and smelled of plywood and drywall dust.

"Thanks for coming over so quick. I'm Reverend Acuff."

"Sure," Nelson shaking the man's hand.

"We've been rebuilding part of the east wing and that's how they musta got in," he said leading them down a hallway where plastic sheets hung on bare studs. A man wearing a dust mask stood sawing a 2x4 with a circular saw. The Reverend raised his hand to him as they passed by.

He yelled over the noise, "Our congregation has been growing a lot in the last three years, and we've started in on some massive renovations. Soon we will be the biggest congregation in the county."

They came to a large foyer with an enormous white cross on the wall and a slotted, literature rack with church pamphlets and pictures of Caribbean orphans tacked to a bulletin board.

"We already have two services on Sunday mornings. Which both of you are invited to," the Reverend smiled.

"So now, does that means you do the same lesson twice in a row?" asked JJ.

"Yes, that's right."

"I appreciate the offer reverend but my wife and her family attend the Church of Christ on Seventh. We've been there a long time. I work with the youth ministry there."

"That's wonderful. The youth are our promise."

"Yessir," said Nelson.

A faint light filtered through the blue stained glass giving the room the feeling of being underwater. A figure came and cupped their hands against the dimpled windows to see inside the church. Nelson tapped JJ on the chest and pointed.

Reverend Acuff walked across the long foyer and opened the door. He spoke to someone then turned to let them in. Winston entered shaking his umbrella.

"Goddammit," said JJ.

"JJ, we're in a church," whispered Nelson.

The Reverend turned on the foyer lights and Winston saw them standing there.

"Ain't there no getting away from you fellas?" said Winston.

"Do you all know each other?" asked the Reverend.

Together they said, "yes."

"Go on in, I'll get the overheads."

The three walked into a large chapel with a vaulted ceiling. Their footsteps rang on the cold herringbone hardwood. The wood pews were lined with plush red cushions. Above the iron caged drop lights clacked on one section at a time, from the back to the front, finally illuminating the podium on the stage and the baptistry. Behind the podium nailed to the wall hung three dead cats.

"Damn," JJ whispered.

"Oh my God," said Nelson.

Winston crossed himself.

Stretched and stapled to the wall, crucified. The circle of fur along their bellies and genitals missing. Tiny stitches created black likes like marching ants along the exposed pink skin.

"Nelson, let's get pictures before anything else. I'm gonna go get the story from the Reverend. Winston?"

Winston looked at JJ.

"Don't touch anything."

JJ met the Reverend as he walked down the long aisle with his head hung.

Nelson and Winston approached the podium, Winston a few steps behind, scanning the brutalized corpses.

"What in the world is going on, man? Why are there murdered cats everywhere?" said Winston.

"Winston," said Nelson. "Hush."

"This is sick. Some straight-up Satanic shit."

"Winston," said Nelson. "What's that on your shirt?" Winston looked down at his shirt. Nelson popped him on the nose with his index finger. "Ah, gotcha. Oldest trick in the book." Nelson brought his camera up to his eye and focused the lens on a cat. "Lighten up buttercup. These people need to see we're in control."

Winston nodded and walked up to one of the cats, reached out to touch it.

"Ah, ah, ah, no touchy just yet," Nelson said.

"It's just like last time," said Winston. The cat wore an agonized snarl, and blood was dried in its nose. Winston caught a whiff of it and turned a little green.

"No, no, no," said Nelson, and Winston bent over.

"You gonna be sick?" said Nelson. "Go, go, go out of here, man."

Winston ran down the stairs cupping his hands to his mouth and pushed aside door open with his back and went out into the rain.

JJ and the Reverend turned to watch him exit.

"Everything ok?" called the Reverend.

Nelson nodded and held up his hand, "Uh...yeah...kinda sorta..."

The Reverend waved and turned back to JJ. "I came in early to my office to write this week's sermon and needed a break and I got up and I usually walk in the chapel to get inspired and I hit the lights…" The reverend removed his glasses and pinched the bridge of his nose. "And I found that. Called the police right away. Then turned out the lights and locked the doors. I didn't want to disturb anything."

"Any ideas as who would do this? Any members that might be upset with you or your church?"

The reverend looked sad and lost for a second. "No. I don't know. I think I need to sit down."

"That's fine...sure." JJ called to Nelson, "Got them pictures, Nelson?"

"Finishing up!"

JJ left the Reverend collapsed on a pew and walked down the aisle toward Nelson. "Come here a sec, will ya?"

Nelson put the lens cap back on.

"Well?" said JJ, quietly so the Reverend wouldn't hear them.

"It's the same. There's no blood and more stitches. Didn't get in real close. Thought you better look before we get them down."

"Alright. Shit. What happened to Winston?"

"I'm not sure. He might be throwing up out there."

"Jesus Christ. Ok. You wanna go talk to him?"

"The Reverend?"

"Yeah."

"And Nelson?"

"Yeah?"

"Don't talk about Satan."

"Got it."

JJ pulled up a deacon's chairs and studied the green thread stitching that bound the cut skin. JJ followed the stitches around the front and to the back. He pulled the cat away from the drywall. A little dampness underneath. He let it fall and leaned back to get a look at all of them together. Each cat was a different color and the black one in the middle. A grey and a calico the thieves on its side. JJ rubbed his gloved finger along the exposed rib of the grey cat.

"Well, what say ye?" Nelson said from right behind JJ.

"Ahhh." JJ jerked to keep his balance. "Jesus, Nelson."

"Sorry, boss."

"Some deranged minds at work here. Somebody with real problems. I don't think we want this in the paper, but it'll be hard to keep this from getting out."

Nelson shrugged.

"Pull up a chair and let's see if we can get them down."

Winston, wiping his face from yuck and rain, strolled back into the lobby and stood for a second next to the Reverend who sat with his head in his hands.

"I never thought I'd see the day when Irontown got a serial killer," Winston said.

"Seriously," JJ muttered as he pulled a staple out of the matted fur of the black cat. "Winston, get the hell out of here."

"I want to help catch him, JJ."

"It's cats, Winston. Cats. Not people."

"Still murder, ain't it?"

Nelson turned from the wall holding the stiff cat in his hands, "He's got a point, JJ."

JJ jumped down from his chair and grabbed a black plastic bag and held it open for Nelson to drop the carcass in. "Alright, Winston, you wanna be helpful? Go write up a report. Put it all in there. Do the research, you get me? Get this thing figured out, so we can put together a profile on this Satanic murderer."

"Seriously, Forte. You'd want me to do that?"

"Heck yeah, we need all the help we can get."

A look of pride and determination came over Winston. "I won't let you down, JJ," Winston said and left out the side door in a rush of excitement.

"Where's he think he's going?" Nelson asked.

JJ craned his head to see out the window. "I'm not sure."

"We may never see him again," Nelson said.

"Exactly."

"Cold, JJ, very cold."

Nelson moved to the next cat and pulled a staple. "You think this has anything to do with those dogs up at Kindred's?"

JJ sighed, "God, I hope not."

As Nelson slipped the second cat into a black plastic bag, four grey-haired women came whispering and laughing, their footsteps echoing through the chapel. They carried shopping bags and one held a portable sewing machine in her arms.

"What in the name of the Lord's going on here?" one of the ladies said, "Get yer feet off those new chairs."

The others stood speechless, their mouths open in disbelief.

JJ looked back for the Reverend but didn't see him. "Ma'am. This is official county business. Y'all need to leave right now."

"Marcia," said one of the ladies patting her friend on the shoulder.

"Addie, I want an answer as to why these two strangers are standing on our new deacon's cha...." She gasped and covered her mouth with a delicate wrinkled hand. "Oh my Lordy, are those cats?"

JJ and Nelson froze. JJ called towards the foyer, "Reverend? Nelson, think you can do something here?"

Nelson stepped down from the chair and walked over to the women still holding the cat in the bag.

"This is worse than when they stole the videos and vandalized the basement," said Addie.

"Oh dear, this isn't the same, Addie."

Marcia stared at the bag Nelson carried with growing fear.

Nelson smiled, "Now ladies I don't want yall to worry," said Nelson waving them on towards the front of the chapel. "We are investigating this, and we swear we want to catch these sickos real bad. Now, what were you saying about a theft?"

Addie spoke up, "Yes, yes, there was a robbery a while back. What would you say, Connie, a month or so ago?"

"Longer, just before Easter Services, you remember? I wanted to make sure we could get that tape for my grandson who lives in Florida and has...hmmm... backslided."

"Yes, that's right. About Easter. They stole all the video equipment. Brand new stuff too."

"Who stole it?" Nelson asked, putting the cat bag behind his back.

"Nobody knows."

Marcia said in a conspiratorial voice, "Well, we got a pretty good guess who it was?"

"Yes, that's right."

"It was Aaron, Mrs. Lennie's grandson, and his friends."

The Reverend walked up to them smiling and shaking his head, "Are these ladies telling you stories?"

"Oh my, Reverend, what's going on?"

"Marcia, we've got good people here investigating this, and you don't need to worry about it."

"They were telling me about a property theft."

"Oh, the speakers?" said the Reverend. "Yes, they were new."

"How did they break in last time?"

The ladies looked around at each other with guilty smirks and the Reverend raised an eyebrow.

"Well, it would seem, that maybe, perhaps, one of us left the door downstairs unlocked..."

"Or ajar even," the Reverend said.

"Yes. We, as the sewing group, have accepted responsibility for leaving the door open. But now we double-check it every time."

"I see." Nelson glanced back at JJ still working a screwdriver to get the last cat unstapled from the drywall. "Were you all here last night?"

"Oh, no," said Addie. They all looked at her.

"Addie, dear? Did you lock it?" Marcia said.

"I can't remember if I checked it or not," Addie said and looked at Nelson in terror. "I don't know," she said. "I don't know."

June 1988

One Sunday I spotted about ten turkey vultures in clear skies spinning in the updrafts. I thought I'd peek at what they was after. It don't hurt to look. Turned into a drive with a burnt-out trailer on the property. And now I think of it, that was Ed Baster's place for a while after he and Shirley split. Terribly nice lady. Last I heard, Ed's acrosst the river now. Anyway, I wandered back into the holler a fair piece trying to triangulate with 'em when they started to drop. Came down in a little clearing. Nothing but birds and branches for a minute. They ain't silent on the wing. Leaves and feathers. I snuck up on my tiptoes. Nasty suckers, that acid vomit can burn a rotten road-killt-opossum.

When I got up there I found the most bizarre scene, something right outta Huck Finn. Two teenage boys were hiding behind a tree holding the end of a rope that was tied to a stick propping up an overturned ice chest. And on the ground underneath was five or six thawing trout on a mound of melting ice. Beautiful fish.

"Boys," I said and they jumped and pulled on the rope and the ice chest went down, bam.

The birds left off screaming and carrying on, plum pissed to be cheated outta lunch. Those two knuckleheads turned beat red, and I walked up shaking my head.

"What in the hell are y'all doing?" I said.

They looked at each other and pointed one to the other, their lips working like a largemouth bass but nothing coming out. It got real quiet and you could hear the traffic driving by on the highway and then one of them boys said some 'bout " getting a vulture?"

I said, "Oh, and what, like a pet?"

They said yessir. I don't know that I did a very good job of keeping the grin off my face, but I tried.

"Get outta here," I said. And they said they had to get the cooler, and I gave'em a stern look. They said they stole the fish from their dad's fishing boat and they had to at least get the cooler back or they were dead meat. I said, "dead meat?" They said yeah. I laughed. I told them to tell me their dad's name and I'd return the cooler. When they left their tails were tucked. I went over to flip the cooler and, shit ya not, found this damned bird just feasting in the dark there, its little red wrinkled head digging into the fish guts.

4

They drug the dead man face up by his cold wrists with one eye open and the other half-cocked. His full, hairy belly exposed and still dripping cold from the creek. Above the bridge hung rusted and skeletal, the white Ford Taurus with its door ajar dinging distant in the valley against the running water.

When he had seen the Taurus, he pulled up along the edge of the risers and stepped out onto the ancient wooden planks, and looked down at the black shape slowly bobbing in the water.

A mockingbird screamed at him. He closed his eyes and took off his hat.

He looked over the edge at the forty-foot drop and the current meandering down the deep hills into the Ohio.

An old man fished upstream. The thin silver of spider's silk stretching from him to the dark pool in tree shadows. JJ called and the old man looked up at him. He waved and pointed down at the body. The man's gaze followed the direction of the finger, and he paused to study the currents a moment, then slowly turned back to his line. JJ, a tiny frantic figure above, lowered his hands. The banks of the tributary were covered in bramble and a floor of slick mud. JJ crouched and worked himself down, his hands out for balance. The thick grass caught his buckles and blackberry thorns tore at his pocket flaps. At the water's edge, he stopped and held a hand to shield the rising sun.

The body float face down in a calm shallow pool where rainbow eddies spiraled in the water. Jumping stone to stone, JJ followed the body from the bank, slow-moving in the summer current. He got ahead of it and crossed the stream on a fallen tree. It came on predictable and light, wearing its black blazer soaked a darker black. JJ reached and grabbed him by the collar, the man's empty hands swollen like baby toes. He stepped into the stream and the cold clear water spilled into his boots. He steered him by the shoulders towards the bank and his belt hung on a sunken branch.

Minnows dart over the brown gravel. He pushed on the man's boots gripping them by the rubber soles but the body would not move. When he slipped on a rock he went under for a moment gurgling, the sound below opaque and loud and he saw the man's soft green face underneath staring at the minnows. He pulled himself up by the waterborne legs, gasping, and rubbed his face, breathing heavy.

"Goddamn, you."

Taking the man around the waist he reached under the torso and felt the exposed skin and the belly button there and followed it down to his crouch where the sticks stuck, and he snapped the branch free.

Pulling him by the wrists they reached the bank. His belly squished in the mud as JJ worked him onto land. He left a slick path in flattened grass. When he got him nearly to the top of a grassy hill where an empty gravel road lay he lost his grip on the meaty, slippery arms, and the man slid like a fish down the embankment and pitched and rolled in the water, turning over with arms out.

The bulging brown eye's lifeless stare and the skin with its rubbery thickening in death. He was in his forties or older. His large nose was marked by tiny deep-set blackheads.

The fisherman may have thought it a strange baptism, JJ standing over the man with his hands on his lapels, bobbing him towards land, the dead man's head tilting back, arms out in total surrender. Gripping him under the arms and fishing him half out of the water, JJ sat on the bank, himself half in the current, exhausted. He looked over at the bank where the old fisherman stood watching.

"Howdy," JJ said and looked down at the body. "I saw him floating down here. There's a car up there."

The old man did not move.

"Could ya give me a hand?"

The old man blinked.

JJ looked down at the body.

"He's waterlogged and heavy as a brick."

The old man wore his gray hair down in braids. His skin golden like a roofer's.

"Jumped?" the old man asked.

JJ shrugged. "I don't know. I didn't see."

"I did."

"You saw him?"

"Jumped."

JJ could smell the fishy old man as he neared. They pulled the body up by an arm and got it out of the water. The old man kneeled down and felt for the heartbeat, leaned in to listen for his breath, and began to quietly chant. He closed the dead eyes and hummed and ran his hand in the air above the man's chest and face. JJ fanned a mosquito from his ear and stood with a hand on his hip watching.

After a while, JJ said, "Alright. Cool?"

The old man's eyes were serious. "Put him back in the water."

JJ laughed and looked at the water and said, "What?"

The old man looked up at the bridge. "He was troubled."

"Well, yeah, I'd say that's right."

"Put him back. He's not our burden."

"What? Like hell... He's not our burden, Jesus Christ. Are you going to help me get him up the bank or not?"

The old man looked at the bank, then took hold of the dead man's wrist and began pulling him up. Their heels dug trenches that filled with the lap lap of the current. JJ grabbed the man's other wrist, and they worked.

The old man's overalls were hand patched with loose, irregular embroidery floss, multiple pairs composed into one.

"Are you a policeman?"

"Not exactly. I'm with Fish and Wildlife."

The old man paused and made a face and let go of the dead man's arm and JJ lurched to keep the body from sliding.

"Hold on now, man; we're almost there."

The old man shook his head. "I don't help Fish and Wildlife."

"Now hold on a second, partner. We've got six feet left." JJ grabbed for the old man's sleeve as he went up the bank and the old man shook himself free nor did he look back.

"What the hell, man?" said JJ. "Why not?"

"Your institution is corrupt," he said and disappeared behind the trees. JJ heard it tumble back down and turned to see the body below splash as it hit the water with such force that it went under and surfaced like a cork a few seconds later in the middle of the creek. JJ looked for the old man and trampled through the brush trying to follow the body downstream and back to the water's edge. He emerged from a curtain of vines and disturbed a crane basking in the sun. It entered the air with the laborious flapping of its oversized wings and caught the wind then coast gracefully, sailing along the creek, arched and still.

He was alone. The leaves swayed in the breeze. The body was nowhere only the running water.

Ruddy faced he made his way up the hill to the bridge. And when he finally lifted himself up by a metal strut he found the Ford Taurus gone. His hands on top of his head he walked to where it had been.

"What in the religious fuck?" he said and turned and looked for it behind him at the other end of the bridge. Not a bird, not a car, not a man stirred the rusted hull as it creaked under his soaked boots.

5

At Donna's desk, he leaked creek water on the linoleum. She removed a ballpoint pen from her mouth to look at JJ.

"What the heck happened to you?"

He looked with such an intense stare at the American flag in the corner of the room Donna turned around to see it.

He looked down at her and said, "I found a dead man floating in a creek."

She leaned back in her rolling chair. "What?"

He walked with his boots squishing to the visitor's chair and sat down. Water began to pool underneath him. He rubbed at his eyes with his palms.

"I found a dead man floating down a creek."

"Dear Jesus," she said. "Should I call Ernie?"

He looked out the window. "It's raining."

Donna stood and poured him a cup of coffee and placed it in his hand and stepped back and watched him with concern.

"Should I call Ernie, JJ?"

"I lost him."

"You lost him?"

"I lost him," he looked back at the rain on the window. "He disappeared."

"Do you need a towel?"

She looked out the window then turned back to him.

"I just got a call from Jack Kindred," she said.

JJ put the coffee down.

"Is Nelson around?" he said walking to the coffee on the folding table and taking the sugar jar and tilting it into his cup. Donna watched him. "No," she said.

He poured and paused and poured a little more watching the sugar crystals fall and dissolve.

"I was just up there at the Kindred's place."

He stirred with a spoon.

"I know. I'm sorry. They asked for you specific and all." Donna said.

He sipped the coffee. Stirred some more. Took the spoon from the cup and stuck it in his mouth. Then took it out as if to say something but just held it there.

Donna sat back down at her desk. "Now I understand," she said.

"Understand what?"

"Why they think they can treat you like their personal assistant."

He sipped the coffee.

Donna rummaged through her desk, rattling papers and coins and pens, and, finally, she fished out a little manila envelop about the size of a business card. She opened the metal flaps and then turned it upside down. The key to his drawer fell into her open hand. She stood up and took it to him.

"Here," she said and took the spoon from him. He took the key and looked over at the rain on the window.

"It's raining."

The picture of his father stood in the half-light of his office. He closed the door behind him. His father gripped the top of his wooden office chair and that same American flag in the lobby was in the photograph behind his dad. JJ changed into a dry pair of pants and hung his wet socks above the vents to dry.

He walked out with a paper sack and put it down on the desk in front of Donna.

Donna looked at him and slowly reached to peek inside. JJ sat down in the rolling chair in front of her desk.

"Dang," Donna said.

"Yeah."

She took out a stack of rubber-banded twenty dollars one inch thick.

"How much is this?"

He sat his coffee down on the desk. "Ten thousand nine hundred fifty-four dollars."

She blinked.

"Thirty percent over fifteen years."

"Jesus." She reached and fumbled around in her purse and came up with the key to JJ's desk and held it up to him.

He put it in his pocket.

"Thanks."

"Today's the day you agreed to go to the high school. Remember?"

"Fuck," he said. Then to Donna, "Sorry for cussing. That's today?"

"Yep."

"Motherfucker," he said. "It's gonna be a helluva a day, Donna."

"What are you gonna do?"

He looked at the ceiling and sighed. "I'm gonna go out there."

He patted his pocket for his keys and stiff-armed the front door and passed into the rain.

"Hey, JJ?" Donna called. "You want this coffee?" He was gone. She picked it up and took a sip and grimaced. "God, that's terrible."

6

Despite the rain, he rolled down his window and told the dogs to hush. They nipped at the back tires, barking. There were so many trucks and cars parked along the drive he pulled in beside one of the trailers. A group of young men stood under the porch of the cabin smoking and eyeing him with their arms crossed.

"Hey," JJ said, "Jack around?"

A kid in a cut-off Metallica t-shirt and long blonde hair looked at him and pulled on his cigarette. He stepped forward and blew smoke and said, "He's busy."

JJ smiled at him. "Jack's the one called me."

"Come back later," he said.

JJ looked around at the others staring at him with dead indifference. "I ain't coming back," he said to the boy.

The cabin door opened and Bullet clomped out to the porch putting on a jacket. He smiled at JJ and pat Metallica on the belly. "Okay, okay, Carl, I'll take it from here."

"What's going on, Bullet? Ya got some more dead dogs for me to look at?"

Bullet's cigarette hung from his lips and he tapped the ash off with a weird fish-like movement of his mouth.

"Forte, why you gotta be an insensitive fuck all the time? I didn't wanna call ya, but Daddy said we had to. Follow me. You boys get on." The gang went walking off toward the school portable. Pulling up their shirts against the rain.

"Fine new welcoming committee," said JJ glaring at Carl as he passed.

"They're kids, Forte," said Bullet and pointed to Carl, "that'n's mean as a snake."

Jack's cabin was a patchwork of wood from different sources. Reclaimed shacks and roofs standing on mammoth wooden beams. JJ followed Bullet up the wooden staircase. Bullet opened the front door and slid his boots off and put them at the end of a long row of shoes. Mud covered hiking boots, a pair of children's tennis shoes, red high heels, and a fine pair of alligator skin cowboy boots.

"Leave your shoes," said Bullet.

"I don't plan on staying long, Junior. If it's all the same to you, I'll keep'em on."

Bullet took the cigarette between his fingers and blew the smoke behind him.

"Forte, I ain't gonna have you track mud into my father's house."

They stood staring at each other. Bullet put the cigarette back in his mouth and gestured his chin at JJ's boots.

JJ sighed and knelt.

"You know how many germs are on your shoes? American culture can be so god-awful backwards. Eastern folk been removing their shoes for plum near four hundred years. Smartass."

Bullet led him through a long dark hallway with high ceilings where laughing voices and clinking glasses echoed. They came to a set of large wooden double doors and Bullet opened it for him. Lavishly decorated with a deer antlered chandelier that gave off a soft warm light and huge bulbed lamps sat on wooden tables glowing pink. JJ stepped inside and walked across a bearskin rug. Jack sat at the head of a long table with a group of men and a woman smoking and playing cards full of empty glasses, bottles, and their full ashtrays. Among them, Reverend Acuff gave JJ a nod. A Chinese man in a velvety black blazer stood up with his hands clasped formally at his waist and bowed to Bullet and JJ, Bullet waved him back down. The middle-aged woman wore a dark dress with a daisy pattern on it, her dyed blond hair up in a bun. She turned and looked at JJ with a drunken smirk.

A few feet beyond the gamblers, stationed lone in the large room, sat a young man bound with ratchet straps to a ladder-back chair and a handkerchief gag tied around his mouth, his eyes widening, hopeful and desperate, as he studied JJ's arrival. A small old woman was vacuuming the green carpet around the young bound man's shoeless feet, and he lifted his right leg so she could get it underneath him. His other leg was wrapped in towels stained with blood bound together with duct tape.

Kindred rose to meet JJ and yelled to the old lady, "Shut it off for a moment, Granny."

She turned and smiled at Jack and cupped a hand to her ear, then saw JJ standing there and smiled and waved at him.

Kindred drew rapid circles in the air with his large index finger. She went to the wall and bent and unplugged it, and came up to them winding the cord around an elbow.

"Can I get you, fellas, anything?" she asked.

"Um...No mam," said JJ.

"Jack?"

"I'm fine, granny."

She wheeled the vacuum out of the room. Along the wall was a series of mounted ducks, wings spread, and an empty leather couch that spanned twenty feet.

"Forte, Forte, Forte. I'm glad *you* are here," said Jack Sr. coming around the table to greet him and took JJ's hand in his. JJ stood shocked at his size, his two hands engulfing JJ's. The size and texture of his fingers like a baseball mitt.

"Is that right?"

Bullet sat down at the table and Jack put one big arm around JJ's shoulders and led him towards the bound man. "We trust you, JJ. Just like we trusted your Daddy. You've had some big britches to fill. Your father understood spirit. And in the spirit world, the law is a bit..." Kindred held up his hand and teetered it side to side, "wiggly. Justice and law are different things, don't you think?"

"What have you done, Jack?"

Kindred winked and smiled. A canine tooth was missing. A dark hole.

"Caught a trespasser."

"You did this to him?"

"He done it to himself. Poor boy stepped in a bear trap."

"Shit, Jack."

"Ah, it ain't that bad. My granddaughter fixed him up. I don't think it's even broken. We give him some whisky to help with that."

"Why ya calling me and not the sheriff?"

"He was hunting on my land, JJ. Hunting. That's you. And he had others with him, but those heroes ran off and left him."

Jack turned to the card players. "Friends is all we got in this life, ain't that right, fellars?"

The card players held up their glasses.

"You said it, Jack."

"Here, here."

The Reverend nodded and said, "I say Amen to that, yessir, a man's companions are..."

"Untie him, Jack," said JJ.

"Askt him a question first."

"I'll question him at the Sheriff station."

"Askt him what he was doing."

The gagged man looked back and forth between JJ and Jack whining through the gag.

JJ rolled his tongue over his teeth and looked into the man's wild eyes.

"Untie the rag."

The man followed Jack with his eyes as he went behind him to unbind the knot. When the gag was removed the man leaned down and smacked his lips and rolled his tongue around his mouth to wet it then looked up at JJ.

"Gaaawdamn. My leg is paining me something awful," the man slurred.

"Is he drunk?" JJ asked.

"I give him a little whisky for the pain," said Jack. The men around the table snickered.

JJ looked back and said, "You're okay with this Reverend?"

The others looked at Acuff and he said, "Well," he cleared his throat, "It's unfortunate."

"Unfortunate?" said JJ.

Jack poured another shot of whisky at the table and walked it over to the bound man saying, "I couldn't agree with you more Reverend. I couldn't agree with you more."

He waited for JJ to move out his way and then stepped in close to the man and fed him like a mother bird.

"Colon cancer is unfortunate," JJ said. "Tornadoes are unfortunate."

"Yes, well," said the Reverend. "The pain of this life is..." he paused to think and belched and said "excuse me" then went on. "It's temporary compared to an eternity with the damned." The reverend found his train of thought, "This is merely malcontentment amongst the wicked of this wrecked and ragged earth. But as the good book says," the reverend said turning to the men at the table, "that which don't kill us makes us stronger."

"Here, here," the men raised their glasses and drank.

"How long have you had this man strapped to a chair?" JJ said.

Jack thought for a moment and smiled, "I'm not sure," he said. "We've been going all night."

And the men raised their glasses.

"I wanna press charges against this man," the young man said.

"Well, well," said Kindred and looked at JJ with surprise. "I declare. Can you believe that, Officer? After all this nursing we done give him?" Jack looked to his friends at the card table and raised his eyebrows in questioning. JJ turned his attention to the man.

"What's yer name?"

"Bennett."

"Bennett what?"

"Stofka."

"Ah, a Czech," said Jack.

"What are you doing on Mister Kindred's property?"

"I didn't know it was his."

From behind JJ Jack leaned in and said to the man, "I own everything for miles and miles, son. From here clean to the State Forest. He had this crossbow on him, too, Officer Forte."

Jack showed JJ a high-powered crossbow with a scope the diameter of a fist.

"If you were in the Wayne National Forest with that you are in for some trouble. That's a wildlife refuge."

"We was huntin' boar," the man said through his teeth.

Jack laughed. "Forte, this would put down an elephant."

"He's right," said JJ. "Wild hog doesn't go out of season..."

"Come on now, Forte, you're sharper than that. Ask him what he was really hunting?"

"Please," the man pleaded to JJ.

JJ bent down to look at the bandages and duct tape. He pulled at a bent corner and the man grimaced and said, "Fuck, God!" Underneath the skin was red and puffy and blood seeped from the giant teeth marks the trap left in his flesh.

JJ stood up. "Alright Jack, enough, help me get him to the car."

"Of course," Jack said with a little bow and turned and snapped his fingers at Bullet. "Gentlemen, excuse us a minute. We'll be right back, and the game will go on."

They pulled out of the hollow with the man in the back seat swaying drunkenly.

"It smells like skunk back here."

They looked at each other through the rearview mirror, JJ didn't say anything. They turned left on the state highway and Bennett asked, "Where we going?"

"The hospital and then the Sheriff's."

He sat back and said, "Can't we make a deal?"

JJ looked back at him. "I'm pretty sure we already did."

Bennett hung his head.

"What were y'all hunting up there? I'm not buying the boar hunt bullshit," JJ said.

Bennett was quiet. JJ saw him belch. He held his eyes closed for a second and then he opened them fisheye wide in the dark and he continued to sing,

"You seem in pretty good spirits for a guy just almost died."

"Oh my poor Shelly, She wishes we would marry, I hunt alone by the tributaries, brought her a dowry, the finest dead deer, now her heart belongs to Edward Belvedere."

"What'd you see, Stofka?"

He wiped his mouth with his sleeve. His eyes blinking slowly.

"Let me go. I'll tell ya."

"Dudn't work like that."

The man looked out the window.

"I saw a bear."

"Black bear?"

He shook his head.

"Weren't a normal bear."

"No?"

JJ drove with the lights flashing but no siren and cars pulled over to the shoulder. "What was it?"

Bennett leaned his head against the glass.

"What was it?"

The man grinned and drool dripped from his mouth.

"Damn you," said JJ and shook his head.

"JJ?" buzzed the cb.

JJ locked eyes for a moment with Stofka in the rearview mirror.

"Yeah, Donna," he said.

"Are you still headed to Colleen's class at Greene County High today?"

"Fuck," said JJ. The man wiped his mouth with the back of his hand and studied it.

7

His words echoed in the high ceilings where the rafters crisscrossed and huge nails hung down like metal claws. "Did somebody have a question?"

The students sat arranged on the gym bleachers giggling; a girl pointed at a boy on the front row, his mule teeth glaring as he grinned. Above the gym, lights buzzed with a constant electric hum, and the fans turned slowly, sloshing the hot afternoon air around.

JJ took a step forward. "Did you have a question, son?"

"I said yer mom's a wild animal," said the boy and smiled and looked around at his peers, and the other students laughed.

"My mother's dead," JJ said.

The gym went silent, and they looked at the big tooth boy, and he didn't say anything more. Colleen, the gym coach, a blond woman in shorts and a whistle that hung around her neck said, "Jessie!" and then mouthed *I'm so sorry* to JJ. JJ shrugged and opened his carrier and hooked a leash onto the raccoon's collar. Rascal poked his head out and sniffed and some of the students gasped, and a loud cacophony of voices bounced around the gym.

Colleen stood and yelled, "You all listen, or we will end this so fast it'll make your head spin. Tom, you get that gum out of your mouth."

"Can we pet him?" a small black girl asked the gym teacher.

"Not right now, Cassie," said Colleen. "We've got to be quiet or you'll scare the animals, ok?"

JJ let the raccoon grab his shirt and look around.

"Unless you see them in a place they shouldn't be, you should leave wild animals alone," JJ said.

Standing in the back to get a better view, a boy asked, "Like where?"

"Well, Rascal was found clinging to a sewer drain. When my friend Nelson saved him he said he looked like a little bandit behind bars." The raccoon looked up and stretched a paw and touched JJ's chin, then climbed onto his shoulder.

"Wild animals have one rule," he said to the kids. "Stay alive."

"Like the law of the jungle?" Her braces and glasses reminded JJ of someone he used to know.

"Sure. Yeah. Like that."

A boy shouted from the back, "So you shouldn't have them wild animals here at all then right?"

Rascal wouldn't let go of JJ's collar, and he had to pry off his little fingers to get him on the ground. "These are animals that needed a little help. We rescued them. And while they recover from stuff we did to them, we use them for education."

"What'd you do to them?"

"No, I mean humans. Stuff humans did to them."

Rascal stood up on his hind legs and walked a few feet. The kids' eyes grew wide.

"Were they tortured?" The girl with braces lisped.

"No. I mean that they were hurt because they were caught up in the human world."

"Oh." The girl said.

JJ walked Rascal on his leash around the gym in tiny circles and then scooped him back up. "Anybody want to pet him?"

Their hands shot up. "Okay, okay...I'll bring him around."

The kids took turns rubbing their hands down Rascal's back. The raccoon hung to JJ tightly. His eyes slowly closing.

"I think he likes it," Colleen said to JJ.

"Yeah, he's a con artist, for sure." JJ took the now sleepy Rascal and put him into the carrier.

"Okay, now y'all wanna see something really cool?"

A boy with long brown hair chewed on his fingernails. A domino effect of yawns passed through the kids. A tall girl with side ponytails and a tall dark-haired boy held hands and the girl in the seat behind them tapped her friend on the shoulder and pointed.

He put on his giant leather glove and removed a blanket from the next carrier and pulled out the owl. One boy's mouth fell open, and he looked around at his classmates and slapped his neighbor on the shoulder and pointed. It blinked its taxi-yellow eyes.

"This is Dexter, a Great Horned Owl. That's the biggest 'eared' owl in the U.S.A."

"You mean like the world record?" The owl took the children's stares with stoic resignation.

"No, good question, it's just the biggest type of owl in the nation. Dexter is actually kinda small compared to some of his sisters. He was found caught on a barbed-wire fence."

The owl turned and blinked.

"Nothing scares him," JJ said. "He'll eat everything from mice to snakes to turkeys, even skunks--"

"How do you know it's a boy?" a teenager asked.

"--even porcupine." JJ stared into the huge glass eyes. He could see his own reflection in them, warped and stretched as in a funhouse mirror. "They'll push out other predators, invade woodlands, destroy populations. They don't have mercy." His chin wore a five o'clock shadow and his eyes were wrinkled and his hair a mess. "Nothing can be done to stop them." Colleen was staring at him with concern, and the children were beginning to whisper to each other.

She stood up. "How do you know it's a boy owl, JJ?" she asked.

JJ looked up at her. "The males are smaller. But just as deadly. They can see expertly at night. And they can rotate their heads about 270 degrees. They got these little mirror-type things in the back of their eyes that boosts their sensitivity to light. They are on their prey before they even know it."

She smiled and nodded. JJ looked at his watch.

He put Dexter back and draped the blanket over his cage. She came and whispered, "Are you okay?"

"Fine," he said. "One more," and opened the Hawk's carrier and let Percy onto his glove. He attached her wire rig and removed her black leather hood. She glared at the kids on the bleachers with her bird's indifference, and they sat in dumbed silence watching her.

"I'm gonna show you guys how I feed Percy. See her eyes and her beak and streamlined feathers? She's made for speed. Her eyesight is so good she could see a bug crawling on your shoulder from across the gym."

He sat Percy on a perch and took a thawing mouse from a cooler and held it in front of her nose, then backed up holding the mouse out in front of him. The students held their breath. He threw the meat and it spun in the air, its pink mouse limbs spreading, and Percy watched it drop onto the glassy gym floor with a slap. A kid laughed and the students looked from the bird to JJ.

"Come on, Percy," he whispered. He picked the mouse up and walked back to his position.

"One more time," said JJ. He tossed it again. It spun, the dead mouse with eyes closed. The students craned their heads and followed it up toward the rafters. Percy watched it descend and hit the floor and bounce. Several kids booed and the noise veered off the angular vectors of the gym. Percy leaped and flew wide over the bleachers. The kids speechless watched her circle the gym. She flew one loop and seemed to cock her head to see the kids, then she returned silently back onto JJ's arm.

"That was awesome!"

"Do it again."

The bell rang and JJ could feel Percy start and hunch, and he raised his arm to balance her. The kids got up slowly and filed out of the gym hefting their bags and saying thank you to JJ as they left. Cassie, a tiny girl who only came up to JJ's waist, stopped to ask if she could pet the Hawk. JJ took her hand and guided it over Percy's feathers, and she smiled and gasped in wonder.

JJ put Percy in her carrier.

"JJ, I'm real sorry about that," Colleen said.

"They were fine," he said and waved to one little girl.

"I really appreciate you coming out here. They may act like they don't care, but some of them were really into it."

JJ zipped up Percy's carrier and stood and Colleen was very close to him, and he took a step back. Her eyes were ice blue and slightly distorted by her thick glasses. She smiled.

"Your welcome, Colleen."

"That owl's a little scary."

"He's intense."

He picked the birds up.

"Can I help you?"

"Well, you wanna grab the raccoon?"

She picked up Rascal and held the door for him with the other hand as JJ waddled into the parking lot. She followed him to the truck.

"Oh?"

"Huh?" JJ sat the animals down.

"I thought you were with animal control," she said tapping the fish and wildlife logo on the Bronco door.

"Really?"

"No, I'm kidding. I know ya hate that."

He flipped the tailgate down and put the animals in. He looked around the campus and into the green trees that lead out to the fields.

Colleen bent and held a finger to Rascal's cage and baby talked with him.

"I know he looks like a teddy bear but his teeth are sharp."

"Really?"

JJ looked at his watch. She leaned against the Bronco and took a pack of cigarettes from her pocket.

"I try not to do it when kids are around but..." She put one between her lips and offered the pack to JJ. He shook his head.

"I know it's unbecoming of a lady to smoke," she said and flicked a lighter and cupped the flame.

"I quit."

"No shit? That's great, JJ."

"Sometimes wish I hadn't."

"Stuff will kill you," she said, letting the smoke curl out of her mouth.

"Yeah, ya know dad passed a while back? Lung cancer," said JJ and held his hand up to block the evening sun.

"Oh god," she said and took the cigarette out of her mouth. "I'm so so sorry. It was lung cancer. I forgot. I feel like an idiot."

"It's fine."

"I'll put it out."

"Don't."

She paused before dropping it on the ground.

"I miss the smell. It's nostalgic for me."

She put it back in her mouth.

"I've got a free period."

He looked back at the red brick building and then at Colleen. "I got somewhere I gotta get to."

She said, "You always had somewhere else to be. Ya know, here's a somewhere."

"Yeah," he said and opened the Bronco door. "Sorry. I got a situation needs my attention."

"Nelson catch a mermaid?"

"Something like that," He cranked down the window and closed the door.

"Alright, get out of here."

She cocked her head and handed him her cigarette. JJ took it from her and looked at the faint red lipstick stain on the filter. He took a long drag and blew smoke out his nose and gave it back.

"Keep it," she said. "Maybe we could have a drink with one of these sometime."

She backed up and JJ waved, smoke drifting out of the crack in the window.

July 1988

Last week I went to the Flea Market in Peytonsville and saw that old hermit. That Indian that lives on out near the Romans. Standing at a tent watching a kid play a Nintendo computer game. It's a new game where you shoot cartoon ducks with a plastic gun. The thing was, this old guy wasn't looking at the screen, he was watching the boy. He shook his head and spat quietly. I leaned in and said, "What kind of a world are we living in?" I think I kind of startled him, but he looked over at me and said, "One full of phonies and fakes. Nothing real." There are old farmers at the Flea Market that sit in a row of white rocking chairs they keep along the barns. I know a few of them. Old war veterans some. Seen more of the world than most of their sons and grandsons. Can't keep themselves from condemning the softness and selfishness of this new generation. Some of those guys been out there in the jungles, on the beaches, in bombed-out cities. They seen things. Me, I got burning bodies in my dreams, and I was only a mechanic. The war was practically over, but I got my kicks. Fired a gun. Saw one of those robed monks burn himself up. Such a good photograph. Ole JFK was a big fan of it, then again he still bombed the hell...didn't he, and still got his brains shot out, poor bastard. I turned to say something else to the hermit he was gone. Got the feeling I'd run't him off. That damned game and then me saying anything, worse thing I could have done. Saw his white head bobbing and weaving through the people and out into the parking lot. The kid and the game. A whimpering dog on the screen brought him his dead duck and the kid gloating like he had done something more than squeeze plastic. There's new things coming, alright, but they're all fake, plastic, and simulated.

8

He found a nurse wheeling Bennett Stofka down the hospital hallway.

"How is he doing?"

He was handcuffed to the wheelchair, and he grinned at his reflection in a glass case that housed a fire extinguisher.

"Why don't you ask him yourself," she said.

JJ bent down to look at him. "Mr. Stofka? How ya feeling?"

He drooled. "I'm on a mountain."

"Jesus, what'd ya do to him? I need to ask him some questions."

"He'll be fine in a few hours. He's had a lot of stitches. Didn't you, Mr. Stofka?"

"I could have danced all night. I could have spread my wings."

"He's all yours," said the nurse.

JJ sighed.

The sunset's orange and purple clouds reflected off the opaque, metallic-looking hospital windows. Stofka and the nurse waited at the curb. Stofka watched the lampposts turn on with wonder. When JJ pulled up Stofka pointed at them. His pupils were huge.

"Yep, the lights turned on, it's a miracle. Happens every night."

"This man has been through a lot of pain, Mr. Forte. You could show him a little kindness."

JJ looked down at Stofka for a minute. Stofka nodded.

"I think I got it from here nurse, thank you."

"Bye Mr. Stofka."

"I love you, dear."

She laughed at him and went back through the double automatic doors.

"She's my angel," Stofka said.

"Yep. We need to get you in the truck, think we can do that?"

He nodded, and JJ uncuffed him.

He hobbled to the Bronco and got in the backseat.

JJ drove slow over the parking lot speed bumps.

"Hey, hey. Yer droolin' on my seats, man."

Bennett looked at JJ and held up his middle finger.

"How's the leg?"

"Fuck your mother. I fucked your mother."

"Hey, that's great. Mr. Stofka, what did you see on the Kindred's property?"

"Kindred."

"Yes."

"Kindred."

"Do you remember what they did to you?"

Stofka leaned forward in his seat and put his fingers in the mesh.

"And I saved you. Do you remember that?"

"My leg hurts."

"Well, you had a bear trap cut it almost clean off your body. So, it probably isn't gonna feel great."

"A bear."

"Yeah, a bear trap, remember that?"

The hunter was sweating and his eyes swam erratically in his head.

"If I'm gonna bring anything against Kindred you gotta help me. Do you understand?"

"I understand."

"Great."

"Motherfucking bear."

"Is that what you were hunting back there? What kind of a bear was it?"

"A screaming bear."

"A screaming bear?"

He lay down on the seat and began to sing "You Ain't Nothing but a Hound Dog."

"Mr. Stofka? Mr. Stofka?"

"He's doped out of his mind," Ernie said peeking through the window. Bennett's eyes were watery and half-open and he chewed on his fingers.

"He's saying all kinds of stuff," said JJ. "I think you should let him sober up in the tank and then get a statement before you let him go."

"Nothing to worry about, Forte. I'll handle it. Got a full house tonight, but what's new?"

"Here's his prescription from the doctor. Gets his stitches out in a few weeks. You sure you got room for him?"

"This skinny guy? Pshaw, get out of here."

Novak grabbed Stofka by the arm and wrestled him out of the back, and Bennett groaned as he put weight on his leg. Novak looped his arm around his neck and limped along towards the jailhouse.

"Keep those feet moving, kid, I'm not dragging your sorry ass the whole way."

JJ stood at the Bronco watching Novak stagger the man along.

"A little help, Forte, damn, this guy's heavier than he looks."

The cells in the back of the Sheriff's station were full of bodies. Men with red-rimmed eyes pacing turned to watch them as they came in.

"Mr. Stofka, welcome to the Greene County Correctional Facility...or as we call her, the Tank." Novak stood with the trespasser at the open door to the large holding cell. Stofka grinned as if he'd just remembered a joke. "Back up, friends, this guy might puke or bleed on ya."

The prisoners shuffled out of Ernie's way as he sat him down on a bench next to a weasel-faced young man with hay and mud in his hair.

"I gotta get my phone call, man. I get a call." The young guy said, his eyes blazing with energy. JJ recognized him from somewhere but could not place him.

"Ain't my concern, dude. Sleep on it."

"I gotta get my call, man."

"You believe this guy, JJ? Gotta make his call. Gotta call your banker? Got some pressing stock tips to trade? What are we running, a resort?" Ernie turned to the kid. "What are you in for again?"

"They're accusing me of taking meth, man."

"Oh yeah? I think they might be onto something. Look at your big bloodshot UFO eyes. Sleep it off, kid."

Stofka traced the whorls of the wood grain in the bench with his index finger and seemed to derive pleasure from it.

A man with an eagle tattoo across his bald head the screaming beak directly in the middle of his forehead sat with his hands on his knees eyeing Stofka.

"This guy retarded or something?" he said.

Stofka looked at the man and then at Ernie.

"Something like that," said Ernie.

Men with skulls grinning on their biceps. Snakes handling their forearms. Muscles that came from work, not the gym. JJ rubbed his face and caught the eagled man's eye and took a step back. The guy grinned and laughed quietly.

Ernie closed the cell and locked it.

In the next cage sat a middle-aged man in a gray suit with a bag of ice on his neck and another on his crotch. His eyes were puffy, swollen scratch marks ran down his jowls. He gave JJ a look of desperation. There were two men playing cards beside him.

Ernie said, "Come on, Warden. Let's get out of here and back to *freeeeedom*."

"Warden, you the warden, man? I got a complaint about this place." The man with the ice shouted.

"Yeah, me too," said the guy with the Eagle on his head.

"Nice try, dipshits. He's the *Game Warden*."

9

The weight of his body felt new, and he experimented with moving his legs just to see how they worked. From the windows in Kindred's cabin came shafts of light shining into the dense cloudy night sky. He mounted the stairs two at a time, long and curving up to the porch, where intertwining serpents intricately carved into the wooden risers undulated. He looked closer and found etched golden letters forming and disappearing on their scaled bodies. Messages from King James.

We look for salvation, but it is far from us.

Yellow light pulsed at the slit in the bottom of the door. Through the bubbled glass of an oval window, he saw smokey figures dancing to ragtime piano. JJ knocked and the music stopped. A shuffle of tiny feet came across the wooden floor. When it opened the old smiling granny stood there with a plate of cobbler offering it up to JJ. He stuck a finger in the cobbler and sunk his arms to the elbows in the warm, sugary muck. She stood grinning. He removed handfuls of hot slather. She beckoned him inside.

Inside was a saloon filled with tufted circus tent walls where old men sat, their long cigarettes steaming. One nodded to him and the music started up again. Dancing women pointed their long fingers at the smiling old men. Their tanned legs slid between spinning dresses of silk and lace. Their mouths agape with stained teeth like sunken tombstones. Gold and silver fillings humming with their lust. A man draped in a bearskin rug sat alone in a corner, nursing a cigarette. A glass chandelier hung from the rafters, its teardrop shapes refracting diamond rainbows.

Bullet sat at the piano in a red and yellow kimono singing in a clear baritone. His lovelorn voice floating up into the hazy ceiling and his hands flowing along the ivory keys while Koi fish swam on his silken arms towards yellow sunsets. His breathy voice bent the last long and drawn-out word of the song, *"I am bound for the promised land. I am...."*

A cricket sat on a stage built of a stack of leather books and was playing a tiny banjo. Strumming and stridulating with hind stick legs. And cheers filled the room. Bullet smiled at JJ and held aloft a glass of flaming cowboy bourbon and drank. Jack gave burning candles to the girls and rocks to the boys and when they flipped the stones there were fossilized skeletons and Jack named the fish or insect that was captured there until the universe would melt them away again. He named them in Latin and told them about the points in the heavens that corresponded and the candles moved about the room like stars. Jack embraced JJ, touching his forehead to his. His eyes black and speechless and bovine staring out of his huge skull. He released him and stamped his feet and the others circled around clapping and stamping in rhythm. JJ found he was holding a velvet red cape. Jack's fingers, like horns, extended at the sides of his temple, he ran toward JJ and JJ feinted and passed the cape across his huge back and Jack stopped and stood up tall. He bellowed low and deep. A rumble. *olé olé olé.* Everyone laughed and stomped. Grinning, he clapped and joined in the circle singing with his kindle of children.

What say, JJ? Bullet said from JJ's elbow.

I am bound for the promised land.

Me too, brother, me too.

JJ opened a heavy wooden door and a woman and a man were putting on their clothes and turned to look at him. He said he was sorry and closed the door and opened another and a man sat there tied to a chair bleeding out both his ears, the blood hot and glowing like lava. JJ gasped. A lightning bug flared on the man's lapel.

It was dawn. Rain tapped at his window, and he swung his feet onto the carpet and rubbed his face awake.

10

JJ pulled into the Save-A-Lot parking lot. A skeletal woman walked across the tarmac pushing a cart of groceries and dragging a plump little boy behind her. She smoked and glared at JJ as he passed. He parked the truck and took off his Fish and Wildlife shirt and tossed it on the steering wheel and put his gun and knife in the locker he kept under the driver's seat.

At the meat freezer laid the groupers with their black glass eyes and glistening scales. Fillet of fatty catfish and a rainbow trout with its streak of violet. He rested his forearm against the case and leaned in closer.

"Look at that bluegill." Said a man standing beside him. He wore mutton chops to his chin and looked to be in his early forties. "Ain't that a nice fish?" He smiled. He had a sunglasses tan and wore the shades on top of his balding head.

"It's a good-looking fish," said JJ.

"I'm partial to the trout. I've been doing some fishing up on the river. Bout got that bitch figured out. Caught me a trout yay big. That's a ten-pound trout right there." He held up both hands to indicate the length of its body and the size of its head.

Elevated behind the freezer, the butcher in white smock looking like a doctor coming from surgery.

"Hi, JJ. What can I do for y'all?"

"Hey, Reece, why don't you give me a couple of them bluegill."

"Alright."

"Dude, you're gonna love it," said the man with the mutton chops. He pointed at one of the whole fish shaking his head. "Is that'n a fifteen pounder right there?" he asked the butcher.

"The catfish there?"

"Yeah."

The butcher took down his white mask with his latex gloves on and leaned back a bit pridefully.

"Seventeen."

"It's a looker."

"It's an ugly one ain't it."

"Lord yes."

"JJ, no catfish?"

JJ shook his head.

The butcher slid the freezer open and wrapped the bluegill in wax paper.

"You need anything?" the butcher asked the other man.

"I'm just looking. I come off the river just this morning. Got me a killing. Was just telling him. Caught a bunch of trout."

The butcher printed a little sticker with the price and handed it over to JJ.

"Well, you talking to the right guy. JJ knows a thing or two about fishing."

"That right?" said the man. "Don Gates," he said and stuck out his hand to JJ. "You fish?"

JJ shook his hand. "Some yes."

"And you interested in exotic fish?"

"Sure. All types."

"You're gonna love that bluegill. You get a little white wine and add that to a mustard marinate overnight."

"Sounds great."

"Let me ask you this though," he looked up to make sure the butcher was out of earshot. "Ever had sturgeon?"

"No, I ain't never had sturgeon."

"I was out on the river last night."

"Un-huh."

"Last night mind ya. And I fucking shit you not, 60-pound sturgeon. Fucker's long as a shark. Just begging for it, this fucking fish. I mean just about jumped in my boat."

"That right?"

"Yep."

"Where is it?"

"Hey man," he looked around and popped JJ on the chest. "I'm selling if you're buying."

"I'm in the market alright," said JJ opening his hands and forcing a sarcastic smile.

"Well, I done picked the right man."

"You sure as hell did," said JJ nodding.

"I got it out in the parking lot right now."

"Perfect. That's perfect. Where you at?"

"I parked around the side over there. That's my boat...you can't miss me.
I got a few other things to grab, and I'll meetcha there?"

"Ten minutes?"

"That'll work," the man nodded and turned and walked down the aisle.

The butcher came back to the freezer, watching Don Gates walk away. JJ looked over at the butcher.

"Fish in a barrel," said the butcher.

JJ shrugged and shook his head.

He paid for the fish and walked along the shopping center, peering through windows at the long blank white lit aisles of a liquor store with its glittering bottles.

"Some days, you get all the fun, Officer Forte. Shit," he said to himself.

He scratched his head and spat and went inside. The bell jangled loudly. He waved at the clerk, a small rat-faced man who shot him a salute.

He stared at a pint of Jim Beam and saw Colleen reading the labels on two bottles of wine she held; he said her name in surprise.

She almost dropped one of the bottles and fumbled with it and put it up on the shelf.

"Yeah, hey, I'm getting this one, I guess," she said.

"All tastes the same after a while."

"Yeah, maybe. Hi JJ."

He walked up to the other side of the aisle and spoke over the bottles to her.

"Hey, listen, I'm sorry about the other day. It's been a weird few weeks, and I'm a bit....off my game."

JJ watched her face. She smiled slightly.

"It's fine. You're fine. It was good. They are still talking about that day."

"Oh, yeah? The owl?"

"The dead mouse."

"Oh. I forgot about that."

"Yeah."

"What are they saying?"

She stuck her chin out a little and shrugged. "You don't want to know."

"That bad?"

"Not really."

Winston from Animal Control walked up to Colleen and said, "JJ?"

JJ turned. Winston held the same cheap red Monkeytail wine Colleen had.

"Winston?"

"I found it," he held up the wine for Colleen to see, and said, "Oh, you did too. This was the same stuff we had last time right?"

She smiled at him and glanced at JJ, "I think so," she said to Winston.

"Whiskey, JJ?"

JJ held up his bottle. "Yeah."

He looked at Colleen, but she only looked down at the wine in her hand.

"Forte, it's good we run into you cause I got a bunch of stuff to tell ya. I been doing my research just like you asked. Ain't typed it all up yet, but Colleen was gonna maybe help me with that. Ain't that right?"

"Winston," Colleen said.

"I got a feeling all kinds of weird things are going on in Iron town. Me and Colleen we were driving up near Hanging Rock at sunset the other day and we seen these lights out on the lake. I can't figure what they were, JJ. I mean I think we've just scratched the surface. Tell him, Colleen."

"Well," said Colleen and blushed and looked at her shoes, she grabbed Winston's hand as if to stay him from saying anything else.

"I was gonna call yall up soon and tell ya what I found," said Winston.

"I've been kinda swamped this past couple of weeks, Winston."

"It don't matter. I'll talk to Nelson."

"No!" JJ blurted out, then more calmly, "Nelson doesn't need to hear about the UFOs. Leave it with me or Donna."

Winston leaned in and whispered so the cashier wouldn't hear him. "Bigfoot, Satanists, UFOs, corruption of all kinds, JJ. I think they know all about it."

JJ nodded. "They?"

"You know, the mayor, the governor. Everybody's in on it," he said and twirled a finger in the air. "People think the monsters are here to experiment on us or eat us. You know who the monsters are?"

JJ crossed his arms and frowned while bouncing his head up and down in a nervous 'yes' gesture.

"We are. See they just want to make a buck off of it. It's all economics, JJ, I've been reading. Ask Colleen."

Colleen smiled and adjusted her glasses.

"I just read an article said a black bear gall bladder is worth thirty thousand dollars in China. You can get a Cadillac for a gallbladder, you believe that? Something about the bile, they use in medicine. They farm it. Got these bears in little wood cages, it's awful. You remember those dead bears found gutted out near Oak Grove about ten years ago?"

"Winston," said JJ. "What are you getting at?"

"Look, the point is, we got Satanists sneaking into churches killing cats, sacrificing them to Lucifer, and next thing we know it's gonna be babies, and when they do summon Satan out of the ground, it'll be for money, not love of evil or eternal life, just money," he said and looked at JJ triumphantly. "Root of all evil and all that."

"Satanists, here?" Colleen asked JJ.

"I wouldn't worry about it," JJ said.

"They convene with the Devil all along the river," Winston said. "There's sights up and down the Ohio, I heard. I read it in a book at the library, *Satanists In Your Neighborhood.* I really been all over this thing, Forte."

Winston's hand rested casually on the small of Colleen's back.

JJ looked at the hand and started to edge towards the exit.

"Winston, that's great," said JJ. "You write it up, don't worry Colleen with typing it, drop it off with Donna. I'll read it over and give ya a call. Somebody will call you. Officially."

"Hell, yeah, Forte. We'll get em," Winston said smiling.

At the Bronco, he muttered and put on his shirt and badge. He holstered his gun then drove around to the side of the Save-A-Lot and parked catty-cornered blocking the boat in. The man climbed out of his vessel swinging a fishing pole smiling, then he stopped and said, "Well, fuck me."

11

A sunburnt woman, with the words "No Gods No Masters" tattooed on the back of her neck, stood talking to Mabel through the small circular window in the bullet-proof booth. Mabel always wore blue eye shadow on her long lashes. JJ peeked around the woman and waved. Mabel waved back and said, "What's up, Forte?"

"Ernie in?" The sunburnt woman turned to him and looked him up and down and JJ nodded to her. Mabel buzzed him in and waved him back. "I think he is. You know the way."

"Thanks a million."

"He ain't worth that," she said flashing a grin.

"Not even close."

Two officers rose from their desks to peek over the dividers, and see who it was. JJ raised his hand to them, and they raised one back. The long hallway was lined with large portraits of the Sheriffs with their tenures printed below. JJ rapped on Novak's door.

"Come in, gawddamnit," Ernie shouted. He leaned on his desk talking to two young officers, "...I come down the hill and saw there was a car parked out under the bleachers by the football field. Tried real hard to squeeze it up under there. But I saw it, and I knew it wasn't there when I had been by earlier. I'd just left that party I split up and come down the hill and found this ole car. A new station wagon. I turned off my lights and I drove up right behind it. Windows was all fogged up, man. And I knew. I knew it. Get in here and close the damn door, Forte.

"I called in the plates and it was Jim Jacobs' car. Well, I knew Jimbo had a kid, boy about high school age, and I sat there a few minutes trying to think of that bastard's name."

"Jerry."

"Shut up, Spinelli. I got there eventually."

Ernie rolled his eyes at JJ. "Rookie thinks he knows stuff. What's the first thing I taught you?"

The young officer's exchanged a glance and then Spinelli said, "We don't know shit."

"Egg-zackly." Ernie smiled over at JJ and raised his brows. "So I light the thing up. Spotlight and my Mag. And them foggy froggies start fumbling around, and I went to the backdoor and I opened it up. Guess who it is?"

"Jerry."

"No, Spinelli, now... have you learnt nothing? It was Jim. And I says, 'Jimbo, what the hell?' And I shined my light in there and that sure weren't Elaine. Jim come tearing out of there screaming at me. I said, 'Whoa Jimmy, button up that fly, good buddy.'"

JJ coughed.

"I ain't finished, Forte."

"Yeah, ya are. I gotta talk to your mentor for a minute, guys."

"Spinelli, Rodgers, this is JJ Forte, the Game Warden."

JJ shook their hands. The two young officers straightened their starched uniforms and went out smirking and laughing quietly.

"Why'd you do that?"

"Do what?" Ernie asked with his easy smile.

"Ruin Jim for them."

"Jim moved out when the concrete factory closed. They'll never see Jim again."

"Elaine and Jerry are both still in town."

"Oh shit. Forgot about them."

"Yeah."

Ernie laughed and hit JJ in the shoulder with a little punch. "What can I do you for?"

"I'd like to talk to Stofka."

"Who?"

"You know."

"Not real sure. Who are you saying?"

"Stofka. Kindred's trespasser. Beartrap on his leg."

"Oh, yeah, that guy got picked up. He's gone."

"What?" said JJ. "Why didn't ya call me? I wanted to talk to him. I told you that. God, Ernie."

"Sorry, J."

"Well, what'd he say?"

"Didn't say nothing."

"Can I read the report?"

"I thought you already questioned that guy."

"No. No. No... He wasn't in his right mind. God, really, Ernie?"

"Hey, hey." Ernie made a smug face and raised his arms in innocence. "Don't put this on me, man. You picked him up. You make the report. There wasn't much to it all. I mean we charged him for the trespassing, but that's all we could do. I mean the guy was injured pretty severely."

JJ's frustration bubbled up to his neck.

"Okay...I'll call him. Can you get me his name and number and all that?"

"Sure, JJ. Sure, Mabel up front can get you all that stuff. You didn't get his info at the ER?"

"He was bleeding all over the place."

"Well, sorry, I was the only one here, and it was late when they picked him up."

"Who?"

"I don't know. Some guys. Some people he called. Ask Mabel, she's got the names and everything."

JJ paused. On Ernie's desk sat two paper sacks, their paper mouths folded down into rectangles.

"Sack lunch?" JJ asked pointing at the sacks.

Ernie raised an eyebrow. "Huh? Yeah."

"Two of them?"

"JJ, you feeling ok?"

"Why do you have two sacks?"

He shook his head. "Oh my god, man. I brought in a sandwich yesterday, didn't eat it. I brought in another one today. Two, that makes two sandwiches." He picked one up and held it to JJ. "Tunafish, you want it?"

"What do you know about Elias road?"

Ernie put the sack back down on his desk. He shrugged.

"Timber road. What's to know?"

"Ever been back there?"

"It's been a minute."

"You've gone back there though?"

"Why do I feel like you're pulling rank on me right now, JJ?"

JJ shook his head and ran his fingers through his hair.

"I'm sorry. I haven't been sleeping."

"Yeah? You look it. Get out of here, get some sleep," Ernie said and sat down at his desk. JJ nodded.

"You're probably right."

"I think I am."

"Thanks."

"Mabel will get you that guy's number and everything."

"Ok," JJ said and turned to go, but he stopped at the door.

"Hey, Ernie?"

"Yeah, bud?"

"Ya know, I think I would take that tuna."

Ernie cocked his head then smiled. "Get the fuck out of here, JJ. You really want a day-old, tuna sandwich?"

"I haven't had lunch."

Ernie waved him out.

"I'm famished," JJ walked back into his office.

Ernie put his hands over the sacks and looked up, his face suddenly serious. "The offer's expired, Forte."

They stared at each other. JJ nodded. When he turned and went out of the office, he left the door open behind him.

12

The next morning Donna was not at work. JJ unlocked the doors and raised the blinds and turned on the coffee maker. Rascal was still huddled underneath the hay in his cage and he stretched and yawned when he heard JJ replenishing his water. The hushed owl stood eyes closed on its branch; JJ walked in its cage and lay a mouse on the wood beside it and the eyes opened, alarming yellow jewels, pretty enough to worship. JJ sat down with his coffee and donuts and dialed Bennett Stofka's phone number again for the twenty-second time.

He cradled the phone between his neck and his shoulder and bit into one of the soft glazed, warm donuts.

"Hello?"

JJ sat up and put the donut down.

"Mr. Stofka?"

"Yeah. Yeah."

He rubbed the sugar off his hands then held the phone up to his ear.

"Mr. Bennett Stofka?"

"Yes. What?"

"This is JJ Forte, the Game Warden."

"Oh."

"I've been calling you last night and all morning. You don't answer the phone?"

"I'm busy."

"How's your leg?"

"It's fine."

"Really? That's great."

"What do you want?"

"Well, I guess I was wondering..."

"I'm dropping the charges."

"You're what?"

"I'm dropping all the charges on the Kindreds."

"Mr. Stofka, I don't understand. Why would you do that?"

"Talk to my lawyer."

He hung up and JJ sat listening to the dial tone.

He put the phone back in its hub and paused. He picked it back up and dialed the number again. The phone rang, and no one answered.

The front door opened, and JJ heard Donna's upset voice saying, "You are going to say exactly what you told me. You understand me?" He opened his office door and Donna was marching her youngest son, Thomas, by the arm up to his office. "And if I ever hear about you hanging around that boy again I swear to God you won't ever own a car."

JJ raised his coffee in greeting.

"Okay, okay, mom."

"Hi JJ."

"Mornin, Donna. Howdy, Tommy."

He had curly red hair and dark boxy sunglasses two sizes too big for him and baggy pants sagging below his waist.

"This young man here has something to tell you. And take those darn glasses off."

"Mom."

"Do it."

He sighed and took them off superciliously, then blinked like he hadn't seen light in days and it was painful for him. He folded the glasses and slipped them in his waistband. His pretty blue, unhappy eyes would not look at JJ. His lashes were thick and delicate.

"What's up, Tommy?"

"Go on," Donna said and shook him by the arm and dug her nails into his flesh.

"Ow! Alright," said Tommy dropping his shoulder and pulling his arm away from his mother. "I was hanging out with some peeps over at the abandoned concrete factory. And they were talking about like tagging a church."

He spoke in a low serious voice like he'd been brought before a vengeful Catholic priest.

"Okay," JJ leaned in closer to the boy.

"But then Carl started talking about these cats he killed."

JJ stood up and almost dropped his coffee. "Well, wax my ass."

"Tell him who it was, Tommy."

"Carl Kindred."

"Carl Kindred?" JJ asked.

Tommy nodded.

"Carl Kindred," said Donna.

"Any idea where I can find him?"

"I don't know."

"Tommy!" said Donna.

He rolled his eyes and said, "Weekends I guess they hang out there at night."

JJ took a drink of his coffee, looking at the floor, nodding to himself.

From the Chesapeake overlook he could see the abandoned factory's four cylindrical silos and its crumbling walls. In the distance ran the silent river; the water steel blue in the twilight. Three trucks were parked next to one of the darkened administrative buildings. JJ pulled back onto the road and eased down the gravel runoff that led to the factory. He ran the Bronco sideways to stop all traffic from coming or going and yanked on the parking brake. A mud-covered four-wheeler stood latched with ratchet straps in one of the truck beds. Graffiti covered the administrative building: anarchist symbols, peace signs, and an upside-down star.

Voices came from one of the tall empty silos and there was the faint glow of a fire coming out of the top.

JJ poked his head inside a square opening where a door used to have been and immediately the pressure and air temperature dropped. Their laughter bounced down to him from above and in the half-light, he could see their shadows on the curved walls moving in the flickering firelight. Broken glass and rusted and burned metal bolts covered the ground. A thin, dangerous steel ladder bolted to the concrete led up to their hideaway and JJ took ahold of it, the metal groaned and echoed and the voices above went silent. He climbed, making more racket with each step, looking between his legs at the thirty-foot fall into total darkness. The sandy rust came off on his palms as red chalk. JJ carefully lifted his foot around the ladder loops and onto the floor above made of heavy steel, argyle panels.

Four teenagers stood around a bonfire drinking Miller Light from cans and staring through the darkness at him. A burnt couch reduced to its springs sat in the shadows. One boy unzipped his pants and started pissing in the fire and the hiss echoed and the other boys yelled and told him to go to hell. Embers loosed from the fire rose in clouds of red stars.

He heard one of them say, "Who the hell is it?"

JJ put a hand on his holstered Colt and his flashlight in his other and said, "Howdy."

"It's a ghost!"

"Oh hell, Denny, he's got a badge."

"I told you this was a bad idea."

"Shut up, Smithy."

"I'm looking for him," said JJ walking to the edge of the fire and pointing at Carl Kindred.

Carl wore his Metallica shirt and was holding up his hands in fear. He lowered them and squint at JJ over the fire.

"The Game Warden?" Carl said. "What are you doing here?"

JJ stared at him.

"You not hear me, man?" said Carl.

"First, you're all trespassing. Second, you ain't old enough for that beverage in your hand, and third, I need to talk to you about the Church of God's Hands out on Ivy Street."

"We can leave, man," Smithy said hiding his beer behind his back.

"Yeah, we gone."

"Everybody sit down."

A smirk played at the edge of Carl's mouth. None of them sat.

"I think you need to leave," Carl said. "You got a warrant? You got any authority? You a fucking Game Warden...we ain't fishing, man. Second, we don't give a shit. And third, fuck you."

His friends laughed.

"I've heard some nasty rumors about you and your buddies."

"Oh, oh yeah?"

"Yep."

"Game Warden, is that like animals and stuff?" Denny asked.

Carl and JJ glanced at the kid.

"Shut up, Denny," said Carl.

"Were you all with him when he fucked up those cats?"

"What cats?" Smithy said.

"Mutilated cats in a church and at a banker's house. Had their genitals shaved and cut and their blood drained."

"Nah," said Smithy looking around at the others. "We don't know what you're talking about, do we?"

"What else did you do to them, Carl? Something sexual?"

"What? What the hell, man?"

"How deep are your perversions?"

"Shut up, Forte. You think you're a big man? I'm Jack Kindred's grandson, you punk bitch."

"Did you rape them before or after you killed them? Is this necrophilia and bestiality?"

"I didn't fucking rape those cats!"

"But you did kill them. Didn't you?"

Carl stared at JJ and glanced at his friends who stood with held breath waiting for him to answer. Then he looked back at JJ and grinned. He laughed. The others began to laugh, and their voices caromed off the walls.

"Yeah," said Carl, and the laughter died down. "Ok, yeah," he said to JJ. "I killed them. I fucking hung them up and drained them right over there." He pointed to a dark corner of the silo.

Smithy raised his eyebrows and let out a long "ooooh" between his hands.

"If you touch me, my granddaddy will kill you."

"Why'd ya kill them?"

"Cause I was bored, you dumb shit. I don't gotta tell you nothing."

"Carl, I'm gonna take you to jail someday."

"Yeah, you don't got nothing."

JJ reached in his pocket and pulled out a tape recorder and rocked it side to side in front of Carl.

"See that? That's evidence, Carl. That's your confession on tape."

"Ohhh damn," said Smithy. "He just pulled some spy shit on you."

"That's right, Smithy. If anything else dies, another cat, a dog, a fucking mouse. I'm gonna come, and I'm going to arrest you. You understand? I'm going to personally dedicate myself to finding the worst juvey lock-up center in Ohio, look at me, and I'm gonna pull every favor, every connection I have to fuck up your life. I don't care who your grandaddy is." He left the recorder running and put it back in his pocket. "You got anything else to say?"

Carl looked at his friends. They had again grown serious and quiet. Smithy shook his head.

"You're all trespassing," JJ said to the group. "Leave now, and don't let me see you back here, not ever. And leave the beer."

Smithy was the first to put his beer on the floor and walk into the darkness. They filed out. Carl kicked the fire with his boot and shoved his chin up at JJ.

JJ listened to them cursing all the way down and spread the fire with his boot until he was in darkness. He turned his flashlight on and found one last unopened beer. He popped it and explored the walls as he drank. In a corner, he found a bucket half full of blood.

"Bingo."

After he finished the beer, he carefully carried the bucket down with him. Outside the boy's trucks were gone. On the door of the Bronco in spray paint over the Fishing and Wildlife logo was a crudely drawn penis.

"Damn." He stood shaking his head.

13

The garage door stuck where the wheels had come off the aluminum tracks, and he forced it open making the metal screech. The motion sensor light in the second story eave came on. He shuffled into the garage with his flashlight and moved a cardboard box with his foot. He pushed the folded ping-pong table into a corner.

"Where is it?" He said. Mildew and rot hung in the hot, stilled garage air. He found it covered with a tarp behind a broken wheelbarrow and rolled it outside into the floodlights next to his truck. The hose on the side of the house stretched all the way past his parents Buick to his truck where he hooked it up to the pressure washer. When he yanked on the pull cord the engine coughed and revved but did not start. "Come on, come on," he said and gave it a few more pulls.

He unscrewed the gas cap and flashed his light inside and jiggled the machine. He could hear the dark liquid sloshing inside, and finally, he got it started in a cloud of black smoke.

He left the pressure gun on the driveway and went around the house to turn on the water. When he got back the engine had died, and he yanked on the cord again, but it didn't start. He pumped the primer bulb and did it again and did it several times but it wouldn't start. It was very late, and he paced to the foot of the driveway muttering to himself. He cranked on it several more times and finally went inside and got a beer and came back out wearing yellow kitchen gloves and carrying a bowl with warm soapy dishwater and a sponge. He sat them down on the drive at the door of his truck and drank the beer. Then he began to scrub at the spray-painted dick on the door of his truck.

"Fucking little shit," he said.

He rubbed his shoulder on his ear to shoo away the mosquitoes.

The spray paint was stubborn and only a small amount would come off. After working with it for thirty minutes the best he could do was to fade the balls. He tried working with steel wool but just scratched the logo.

He stood and cussed at his truck. "You fucking mother fucking fuck!"

He clenched and unclenched his fists.

The neighbor's bedroom light came on, and he waved to the silhouette that peaked out the window from behind the curtain.

"Hey Frank," JJ said. "Go to bed, you bastard."

Frank raised his hand and then another figure appeared next to him.

"Hi, Mrs. Duval, sorry I woke y'all," JJ said. They couldn't hear him. He shrugged and waved, and they disappeared behind the curtains. Soon the lights went off.

At the edge of the driveway, he looked up at the stars. He still had the yellow gloves on, and he slapped himself in the face. His face showed darkly in the truck's driver-side window. He slapped himself again.

"Come on, you phony. Come on."

14

A cloud of dust followed as he sped past the dogs and stopped the Bronco just shy of the cabin's morning shadow. The gravel was still popping when he opened the door and brought the truck to a halt. At the windows of the cabins and trailers the Kindreds came to watch, dogs barking.

Jack came out the front door. Half his face was bare and red, the other white with shaving cream. He carried a World War 2 era swing arm razor in his huge hand that he lifted in greeting. JJ pushed the dogs from him.

"Forte." The dust from the car spread out over the lawn lighting up the slanting sun that was shining in JJ's face.

One of the other trailer's doors opened and a diapered little boy bolted down the stairs and around the corner of the trailer and into the brush. A young woman with another baby on her hip stood in the doorframe watching JJ and the dogs.

"Can you call them off?"

From the porch Jack yelled, "Get daawwwwwgs." They hackled, back legs buckling at the sound of his voice. "Get!" They turned and ran. The door behind Jack swung open and a few teenage boys came out and stood leaning on the porch rails. They spat one after another.

"They gone," said Jack.

JJ reached in the truck and pulled out a large brown grocery bag, and dropped it at Jack's feet.

"You bring me some fish?"

"You know what it is."

"I'm sure I do not."

"That's all of it I got. Even some of my dad's."

The razor flipped out and mirrored the sky.

Jack laughed and carefully traced the razor under his chin. "This all you're here for? Shit. I thought something was wrong." He dropped a dollop of cream over the stair rail into the overgrowth. "Forte, why don't you pick those bags up and drive out of here a little slower than you come in. I got great-grandchildren running everywhere you know. I got babies with babies. So get the money you and your father earned and go. Get a drink. Or go back to your job. Surely somebody's shot something they shouldn't have or caught some fish without a license and, hell, it's up to you to stop that fucking terrible shit from happening, right?"

"I'm done. Jack, I mean it. I'm done." JJ turned his back and opened the Bronco door.

"Forte, don't turn your back on me, boy. A man's capacity for pleasure is limited, but his capacity for pain is inexhaustible. You understand what I'm saying to you?"

He shut the Bronco door and sped off leaving Jack standing at the foot of the cabin with the paper sacks at his feet.

Bullet came out of the cabin carrying a plate of bacon and eggs. He leaned over to the boys at the rail, "What'd I miss?"

"Shit fire," Jack said as he picked up the sack of money and turned to the boys. "Get back inside," he bellowed. "Not you, Junior." Bullet snapped a piece of bacon off in his mouth.

"Ow-wight," he mumbled.

ACT THREE

December 1988

Late last night I hit a deer on North Seneca. It was just a doe and I snapped both her front legs. Broke a headlight. Dark. Weren't no cars. Stood in the middle of the highway watching her with my flashlight. I heard hunters I respect say there ain't nothing but hunger and fear in an animal, but she weren't afraid. Didn't try to stand. Didn't fidget as I got close. Must have seen me as nothing less than a God come down outta the light. Why the faithful don't get more lessons from God's wordless creatures I don't know. She had a pretty velvety pelt and her eyes were so big. Eventually, I got the rifle. But I felt suddenly like an idiot, with a small mind. And this deer facing its death without fear. There's no bargaining that went on there. No pleading, no regrets. No. I saw myself for what I was. Shot her and loaded her in the truck. What knocked me back was the job, an automatic sense of "get-on-with-it-James". And there's something monstrous about this, monstrous about men and duty, and monstrous, I suppose, about God.

1

JJ tucked his rifle under one arm and fumbled with his keys, tried his key on the front door, dropped them on the ground, and he cursed himself, and finally got his trailer unlocked. It was dark inside. He pushed everything off his coffee table and laid out his Remington 700. He brought back the bolt and inserted three rounds into the spring-loaded follower and then slid the bolt back and down and sat it aside. Then he took his Colt from his holster and slid the magazine out and counted his rounds and slid it back in and pulled the slide back and chambered a bullet.

His living room curtains wouldn't close all the way, and he took a paperclip and pinned it shut. He paced the floor, stepping over a stack of clothes and kicking a box of junk farther out of the way with each turn. He checked the window again and then sat down on his calico couch, sweating and his left knee bobbing up and down. Outside a big six-cylinder engine approached from down the road then paused, guzzling gas as it idled then fell silent. Car doors opened and closed. He went to the window and peeked into the afternoon. Ice cream clouds hung in the cobalt sky. Bullet's viper rolled along the road and stopped near his driveway, sunlight glaring on the windshield. Then a truck pulled up behind his Bronco blocking him in.

"Shit. Shit. Shit." He shouldered the rifle strap and holstered the Colt, then slid the back door open and went outside. In the backyard young maple saplings grew up around his swimming pool, the water green with algae. Percy flapped her wings.

He clicked his tongue at her, and she eyed him. "I ain't got any food."

Another car door opened and closed. He leaned the rifle against the deck rail.

"I got maybe five minutes on this green earth, but you're gonna get out of here."

He undid the wire on Percy's leg, and she hopped away from her house and bounced down the deck railing to sit there preening at a wing.

"Go on now. Go." She looked up at JJ as he approached waving his hands to get her in the air. She hopped and spread her wings and opened her mouth at JJ.

"Percy, please, go." He shooed at her with his hands and she leaped from the deck. He watched her catch the wind and rise up above the cypress tree. She circled and came back racing towards the trailer. Below her, coming out of the woods thirty yards back, JJ spotted Bullet carrying an assault rifle. They locked eyes and Bullet grinned and aimed his gun at the bird. Percy veered right and flew around the corner of the trailer. JJ grabbed the rifle and clicked the safety and then he heard Nelson say, "Holy crap!"

Nelson came round the corner of the trailer carrying his two-year-old little girl. "J, there ya are. Oh my gosh, I just saw a red tail hawk come within a foot of my face. Did you see that?"

JJ looked down at Nelson, then at Bullet behind him in the woods. Bullet had paused, surprised and confused by Nelson's arrival, and lowered the gun.

"Nearly hit me in the face. That wasn't Percy was it?"

"Holy shit, Nelson," said JJ.

"JJ, you mind not cussing in front of my daughter?" Nelson began to walk up the deck steps. "I've been knocking on your door for the last five minutes. I tried calling, you don't answer the phone on Saturdays? I was picking up this little angel from Grandma's, so I decided I'd stop by. How are ya? Your neighbors having a party or something? They's a bunch of cars out on the road."

"Nelson," JJ whispered.

"Gotta lotta firepower there, chief," Nelson said pointing at the rifle. He paused a few steps below the deck and looked down at his daughter and said, "You know Annie, right, J? Can you say hi mister boss man?" The small girl looked up, smiled, and buried her head back in Nelson's shoulder.

"She's tired."

"Nelson." Down below Bullet had one leg up over the chain-link fence. "What are you doing?"

"I come out here to get ya. Found something that I think is gonna blow your socks clear off."

JJ pushed Nelson and Annie through the glass door.

"Whoa, whoa, JJ. What's got your goat this morning?"

He hurried him through the kitchen with a hand on Nelson's back while he watched for Bullet behind them.

"You living out of boxes? It's like the office in here," Nelson said.

JJ eased the front door open and peeked out. Three men stood outside next to a big truck watching the house, waiting. JJ closed the door. He looked around his living room and back at the porch.

"What ya looking for?"

"Nelson." JJ placed both hands on his shoulders.

"Yeah?" said Nelson, a little perplexed.

"We need to get out of here."

"Well, sure JJ. I mean I come to get ya. Everything alright with you, JJ?"

"I got a lot of things on my mind. I think a drive would really do me good, Nelson."

"Well let's go then, boss. We'll make a day of it."

JJ looked down at the child in Nelson's arms.

"Nelson, can I carry, Annie?"

"Annie? Well yeah, sure, JJ."

The little girl opened her warm brown eyes as Nelson placed her in JJ's arms, then shut them again, content cradled in JJ's arm.

"Let's go," JJ said and stepped outside with the rifle in one hand and the child's arms around his neck.

"Never knew you to be too keen on kids. Want me to lock it behind me?"

"Yes, Nelson. Hurry. Hurry. Hurry."

Nelson locked the door and jiggled the handle to make sure he'd done it right.

The three men glanced at each other. One spit on the ground. They walked down the steps to Nelson's station wagon. Nelson raised his hands to the men.

"Howdy do," Nelson said and smiled politely. "You know those fellas, JJ?"

"Get in the car, Nelson."

Nelson opened the back door and said, "Safety first, little buddy."

He took Annie from JJ and sat her in the plastic car seat sliding her arms through and the buckles over her head.

"Oh my god, Nelson, let's go."

"These buckles are frustrating."

"Nelson."

"Alright, I'm coming. You're a nervous nancy today, boss."

Nelson raised his hand to the men as they pulled into the highway.

"Sorry, Nelson, I just really needed to get out of the house."

JJ watched over his shoulder as Bullet approached the edge of the drive with his gun.

"Well, I can barely contain myself either. When I figured it out I just grabbed Annie and went right for ya. I know I should have called ya on your day off but I was too pumped."

"Oh my God, Nelson," said JJ and sighed and cupped his head in his hands. "Thank you."

"For what JJ?"

He looked at Nelson. Nelson's expression clueless and true. He smiled at him. "I'm just happy to see you, Nelson," he said tearing up.

"Jeeze, I didn't know it would mean so much to you, you're welcome, JJ. I didn't know you were as excited about Bigfoot as I was."

JJ continued to watch the road behind them.

"Begfoo," Annie said.

"That's right, baby, Bigfoot. I figured it out, JJ."

"Figured what out?"

"I figured out where he is. Wanna guess? Guess?"

"Where who is?"

"Bigfoot silly."

"Bigfoot?"

"Begfoo," Annie said.

"That's right, baby, Bigfoot. That old hermit's property, Saylor. Saylor. You know who I'm talking about?"

"Yes."

"All the sightings, what's the common denominator?"

"I don't know."

"Saylor! They're all along the Saylor property."

"Really?"

"Yep. Every neighbor has some story. So you know what I'm thinking?"

"I'm sure I don't."

"I'm guessing Bigfoot must live up around there. Maybe even right there on Saylor's farm, maybe in a cave up in there."

"Ah."

"JJ, if I'm right. I mean. We could be famous. And you, too, little sprout!"

2

They pulled into the office and Nelson unbuckled Annie and brought her inside to Donna. Annie and Donna babbled at each other while JJ watched the road and kept a hand on his holstered gun. He backed up to the glass door of the office and leaned it open and waved at Donna.

"Hey JJ."

"Donna, what are you doing here today?"

"Nelson asked if I might babysit, and I had some thing's I needed to finish up here. Plus Tommy has band practice and I can't stand listening to them scream. And I wouldn't miss an afternoon with Miss Annie. You know I love you. Yes, I do. Yes, I do." Donna put Annie on her desk.

"They making scream music?" Nelson asked.

"Oh, they're teenagers blowing off steam," Donna said.

"I'm like you. I can't do that scream music. You oughta introduce them to the Eagle's. I gotta tape I could give you."

JJ let the door swing shut, and he stood watching the road.

Donna looked at Nelson.

"What's with him?"

"He seem weird to you? I'm not sure. I think he's just excited about Bigfoot."

Donna nodded. "Oh."

JJ went to the Bronco and opened the passenger door and sprung the knob that dropped the glove box. Shifting the papers around inside, feeling between them and along the sides, he found a box of half-empty cigarettes and sighed and placed one in his mouth. It was so old the paper was brittle. He lit it.

Nelson, smiling, paused at the azaleas along the walkway and bent down and took a beer bottle from the landscaping to the plastic trash can and threw it away, then finally to JJ at the Bronco. "Are you smoking?"

"Nelson?"

"Yeah?"

"I'm driving."

"Ok."

They squealed out of the parking lot hitting the curb with Nelson pitching forward and searching for his seat buckle.

They sped north into the sloping hills, slowing on the uneven county roads. Like fingers, the wild grapevines hung in the canopy casting purple shadows over the windshield.

JJ slowed as they approached a closed cattle gate.

An old, very skinny but towering man in patched overalls was driving down the gravel road towards them in a blue four-wheeler. When Nelson saw him he pushed himself up in his seat, gripped the handle on his door, and said, "Well, there's the old conjurer himself."

The man stopped at the gate and climbed off his conveyance, swinging his long legs over. JJ stopped ten feet from the gate and held up a hand to the old man. Saylor took a shotgun from a holster affixed to the side panel and climbed the gate in a studied nonchalance and stood stoic where he landed. His mean eyes watched them from a pair of large metal glasses. His long braided hair salt and pepper.

"Let me talk to him, JJ."

"No...now, Nelson...let me talk."

"JJ, I feel good about this. I can get on his level."

JJ looked back at the old man, sighed, and said *ok*. They popped the door handles, slowly opened the doors, and got out of the truck at the same time.

They approached slowly. JJ took a step around to the front of the Bronco and put the small of his back against a headlight. Sunlight flit in the canopy of green leaves.

"Mr. Saylor?" said Nelson calmly.

The old man didn't speak. Nelson turned back to look at JJ. A crow came cawing out of the trees.

"My name is Officer Nelson and this is Officer Forte. We're with the Ohio Gaming Department. Fish and Wildlife. How are you doing on such a gloriously beautiful day, sir?"

There was no reaction, none, from the old man and they waited a moment for him to respond. Nelson and JJ looked at each other, and Nelson gave a little shrug.

"We don't mean to bother you, and we don't mean you any harm, we just have some questions you might be able to help us with. We've been hearing of some strange sightings coming..."

In a swift motion, Saylor cocked a bullet into its chamber.

Nelson threw up his hands. "Whoa, oh man, oh man," he said and they backed up behind the truck's passenger door. He said to JJ, "Ok, you can try now."

JJ nodded.

"Mr. Saylor. It's with big respect that we've come out here to see you. We know you value your solitude."

Saylor's eyes swiveled to JJ.

"There's been some weirdness around your woods recently, and we thought you might be able to help us."

Nelson shook his head and said loudly, "Saylor, I'll be blunt with you. There's been Bigfoot sightings around your woods since the early eighties."

JJ shook his head at Nelson in disbelief.

"Now, I know you know something, sir. You're gonna give us some information, or we are going to come back with permission to hunt your woods. Now you want that?"

Saylor was motionless. His skin was old, leathered. Like weathered barn wood. His enormous fingers gave a hesitant twitch.

Nelson straightened and shook his head, "Nah, I don't think this is getting through, JJ."

Saylor fired his gun into the air and they got in the Bronco and closed the door.

"Crazy SOB, who knows if he can even talk anymore," said Nelson.

"He can talk," said JJ.

"Well, what do we do?"

The gunfire had disturbed the crows and they were circling and making a racket in the sky. Saylor glared at them but had not moved the angle of the gun.

"I do not know."

They waited.

He did not appear to move.

JJ struck his lighter and ran a finger through the flame.

The car was oven hot, and JJ cracked the windows and turned on the engine to
run the A/C. His eyes swimmed in his skull, and he lay his head against the cool of the driver-side window. Nelson watched a ladybug crawl across the dashboard and over to the windshield where it tried several times to get up on the glass as if some glue on its tiny wiry legs wouldn't stick. Above thin strands of cirrus clouds passed slowly over the trees.

"How long we been waiting?"

JJ looked down at his watch. "About ten minutes."

"Has he moved?"

"He shifted his weight to the left foot."

"I need water."

"I've got some bottles in the back."

JJ leaned his head back and closed his eyes for a moment. He was almost instantly asleep.

3

The forest was covered in green vines, the water wheeling motion of snake tails, the hard shell of a rainbow beetle crawling on scat. A marsh rat ran the length of a branch and on came the sure-footed demon hugging her wings to her chest and dropping. She brought her tail feathers down and, doddering at the last moment, her wings out, talons raised, and the rat with no warning was snatched by her clean yellow claw, the long middle nail piercing through rib and lung. It squeaked and the hawk soared and the rat watched the world fall away with horror.

Oh, hungry mother, I am a mother too, can't you see how I am like you, compelled to eat, compelled to speak, compelled to feed my children.

The hawk cocked its head and answered, *Would you speak this way to the berries or the rocks? Or ask me to eat grass like a cow? I am the wind. You cannot tell me where to go or what to do.*

Under pale velvet skies, she flew over the arched bow of the curving river, quicksilver skin shimmering in hidden currents, wingtip to wingtip yawing with peppered drag. A single feather rattled loose. It descended, graceful in the way only leaves and feathers are.

She dove down to the river, her shadow undulating atop the surface of the water. Up ahead in the green current a body surfaced, face up and pink. Plump with swelling. Blue veins running along the face and neck. A black water spider dead on the ear. Wet grass on the bulbous belly. The arms hanging down in the cold water. Her shadow passed over it in a second, lengthwise from head to toe. The rat sees the upside-down grin, catches the smell of the body. The hawk angles up and her shadow shrinks, the river narrows, the clouds expand. The rat cannot shut her eyes, feels her eyeballs bulging in their cranial caves.

In the top of an oak tree, she swallows the rodent whole. The world stretched before her. Her chest pink with blood.

4

"I think he died, JJ."

JJ opened his eyes and sat up straight and said, "How long was I out?"

"Just a few minutes."

The sun glared off the roof of the Bronco. Saylor was still there. His ball cap low on his forehead keeping his eyes in shadow.

JJ rubbed his fingers through his hair. "Gimme that water."

Nelson handed JJ the bottle. "You've talked to him before?"

"One time."

"What'd he say?"

"Nothing much," said JJ. The old man was still holding his shotgun. "He said 'Let the river work.'"

"What's that mean?"

"You tell me, Nelson."

Nelson looked again at the old Indian. He was made of stone.

"I gotta go home, JJ. I don't think he'll ever move."

The wind tore at Saylor's pant legs.

5

They came into the office with Nelson saying, "It's back there, JJ. I know it. He's protecting something."

"He's a hermit, Nelson. He's protecting his solitude."

Nelson took his hat and put it down on his desk to let his sweaty hair air out. "Well, I'm cuss-all pissed."

Donna raised her eyebrows at him. "Well damn, Nelson."

"I know, and I'm sorry. He's sitting on something out there alright, Donna. How did my little girl do?"

Annie stood on Donna's desk and pulled her shirt up to show off her belly button and Donna tickled her. "She's doing fine. Isn't she, yes, she is. We just changed a poopie diaper, didn't we?" Donna said.

"She's my button."

Nelson bent down and kissed Annie's forehead.

"You want to hold her?" Donna asked.

Nelson shook his head, "You hang on to her as long as ya want, Donna," he said.

Donna put her on her shoulder, and Annie reached up for Nelson and said, "Daddy."

"She took a nap and we looked at the Owl and we fed Rascal. We had a good time. Didn't we, Annie?"

"You ready to go home and see Mommy and Rocky?"

She grinned and shook her head and babbled.

"Ernie called asking for you, JJ."

"He did?"

"Yeah, I told him you might be back this afternoon."

"You did?"

"I told him you might could use a Novak pep talk."

"You said that?"

"I did. Something's wrong."

"No. It's fine. Y'all, get out of here."

"Should I have not said that?"

JJ scratched his head. "It's alright. Seriously, it's your day off. Y'all get out of here."

"Jeeze, JJ, slow your roll, we're going. We're going."

"Slow your roll?" Nelson said.

"My kids say it. Far as I can tell it means 'chill out, dude.'"

"JJ, I say we get a warrant and we go in there."

"Yeah, Nelson. I think you're right."

Donna passed Annie to Nelson and he squeezed her and held her up in the air. He turned around and had Annie wave at them.

"Can you tell Mrs. Donna and Mr. Forte goodbye, Annie?"

She waved at them then buried her head in Nelson's chest.

"Bye y'all," said Nelson.

After the door closed on Nelson, Donna said, "Is everything alright, JJ?"

"Donna quit asking me that. It's your day off. Now, go on and get out of here."

"Ok."

Donna packed her purse and left JJ standing at his office doorway. A police cruiser pulled into the parking lot and Donna waved. Ernie stepped out and JJ watched them talking. She pointed inside and Ernie looked up at JJ through the double glass doors. Ernie nodded, and she got in her car and pulled out.

His hand on his gun, gritting his teeth, JJ stood at Donna's desk unable to move.

Ernie had his head cocked to the side looking down at the penis spray-painted on the Bronco, and he smiled, put a piece of gum in his mouth, and looked back at JJ, pointed at it, gave him a thumbs up. A blue dodge Viper pulled into the lot.

Bullet got out of the driver's seat smoking and raised his hand at Ernie. JJ could not hear what they said. Ernie pointed inside. The shocks on the Viper dipped and corrected as Jack's massive form rose from the passenger door. He came to the double glass doors first.

"JJ," he said, flanked by the other two.

"Jack."

"Put the guns away gentlemen. We're here to talk, JJ. I think we can talk can't we?"

"Sure, Jack."

"Bullet."

Bullet put a leather duffel bag on the desk. "We are returning this to its rightful owner."

"I don't want it, Jack."

"That's the wrong attitude, friend."

"I like the new look Fish and Wildlife is sporting these days, JJ. Pretty radical."

Jack said, "You shouldn't have threatened my grandson."

"Your grandson is a dipshit."

"Ok," said Jack and nodded at Ernie. Ernie took JJ by the arm and lifted his Colt out of its holster and tucked it in the front of his pants.

Ernie grabbed JJ's neck and muscled him around Donna's desk and led him back into his office. He pushed him down into his rolling chair, and Bullet looped two ratchet tie-downs around him and cranked on the winch till JJ sat bolt straight.

"I'm glad you wanted to do it this way," said Bullet.

The straps cut into his ribs and arms. Jack cleared a space on JJ's desk pushing a stack of papers to the floor. He plopped the bag down and unzipped it, then sat his giant form on the table and crossed his knees.

"Want me to gag him?" Bullet asked, taking a roll of duct tape from the duffel bag and tearing a length into the air between his fists.

"No. I want him to talk."

"Right. Right."

"Now shut up," Jack said to his son and reached into the bag and took out a stack of bribe money. Jack paused. He looked over his shoulder at Bullet who stood close behind him, breathing audibly.

"Boy, stand over there," Jack said and pointed to the other side of the desk. Bullet looked at Jack, then bowed his head and shuffled around JJ and Ernie to the front of the desk.

JJ looked up. "Jack..."

"Shuddup," Jack said. "We got to re-access this here deal of ours."

The photo of JJ's smiling father looked blindly into the distance beyond Jack.

"I can forget. I can," JJ said.

"That's good." Jack smiled and tapped the stack of money on JJ's forehead. "I'd hate to lose the years of good feelings we had going."

"I don't believe him, Daddy," Bullet said.

Jack sighed and turned around to his son. "Boy, you were never a good judge of character." He turned back to JJ, "That's yer mother's side coming out in ya."

"Shit," Bullet muttered.

"Son, the adults are talking now." Jack followed JJ's eyes to the picture of Forte Sr. "Ya know, your father was..." he looked down at JJ, " more agreeable than you. Easy going. That's what we want. Nothing's changed. You took our money; now you need to spend it. Buy yerself a speedboat. A wave runner. Have some fun."

He pulled a hundred from the stack of bills. His sausage fingers clean, manicured, milky white.

"Spends just fine," he said then crumpled the bill into a wad. He leaned forward and gripped JJ by the jaw and pried his mouth open.

"Open up, Forte."

JJ slung his head and set his jaw closed. Ernie grabbed him by the hair.

Jack shoved the money in his mouth. JJ spit and it dropped onto his lap.

Bullet walked over and wrenched on JJ's pinky finger. JJ's eyes widened, and he opened his mouth to scream as pain coursed through his arm and throbbed in a vein in his forehead.

"Now, Daddy."

Jack nodded his surprise approval and thumbed the wadded bill into JJ's mouth then worked his jaw to make him chew.

"Swallow!" Jack said. "Swallow!"

When it was done Jack leaned back and wiped the sweat from his forehead.

"Open up."

JJ opened his mouth.

"I say, Goddamn son. Not a lick left."

JJ looked down at his pinky akimbo, sticking up from its middle joint like an extra finger uncut at birth; skin white at the bend.

"Now, we've made a transaction," said Jack standing up. "Money's still yours, JJ. Ya done good."

Ernie released the pressure on the straps and JJ gasped.

"Maybe he's still hungry, Daddy."

"Jesus boy," Jack said and shook his head.

They left him sitting in the darkening office grabbing his throbbing hand. He listened to the Viper's engine shifting into gear on the highway.

The money sat on the desk in front of him. He held his hand up and away from him, careful not to bump it as he stood and got a nearly empty bottle of whiskey out of one of the filing cabinets. He sat back down and cradled it in his arm so that he could unscrew the lid with his good hand. He drank the last of it, and winced and let the heat overtake his throat. Then he closed his eyes and screamed as he moved the pinky back into place. He sat quietly.

In the back, he found some self-adhering gauze and wrapped his hand. The owl was awake, and it stood in its cage watching him silently.

"What are you doing up?"

The owl closed its eyes and turned its head and opened them on the wall with its characteristically intense focus. "Yeah, well, fuck you too, old man."

Outside the crickets were loud. He heaped the money in a pile of stones and took his lighter and watched it burn. When it was going he knelt down and fed stacks to the flames. The thin ash spread in the air like birds.

6

The greenhouse plastic was the color and texture of frosted glass stretched over eight-foot steel hoops. Six of them, each about thirty feet, a mammoth operation. JJ peeked his head inside the entrance flap. Two rows of healthy, tomato plants sat on white fold-out tables with black hoses that snaked into the plastic pots and along the ground. Fans above them silently shook the leaves. JJ jogged down the aisle, his mouth open.

The back door of Saylor's house clapped shut, and JJ dropped to the ground and reached for his sidearm. Through the semi-transparent plastic, a shadow figure passed to the far barn. JJ elbow-shuffled his way to the entrance and peaked out. From the barn came the clanging sound of tools and the old man talking to himself. Saylor emerged carrying a bucket and wearing a full skin, taxidermied bear suit, the head of a bear over his own, its fanged mouth open to expose Saylor's face, his old man chest bare to the air. There was, for a moment, an odd doubling effect: the bear very dead, bobbing along to Saylor's long, loping gait as he made his way to the side of his house to fill a bucket with water.

JJ took three steps from the entrance of the greenhouse with his gun aimed.

"Saylor!"

The bear stiffened and turned off the water and slowly sat the bucket on the ground, then Saylor stood, turned to him, raised his arms, opened his mouth, and came running.

"Hey! Hey! Saylor, don't, don't, hey!"

JJ backed into the greenhouse, Saylor picking up speed, his open mouth matching his animal-eyed other. JJ tripped on the plastic seam at the entrance and knocked over a plant and fell, "You know my father!" he said putting a hand up to protect his face.

The bear-man stopped and lowered his arms. "You're a Forte?"

"I'm JJ Forte. I'm JJ Forte."

Saylor leaned back against one of the fold-out tables. JJ stood and adjusted his shirt and holstered his gun.

"I'm sorry about your plant."

It lay on its side; the plastic cracked and the black soil spilled. JJ scratched his head.

"I wasn't sure you liked my father."

"I didn't like your father."

"Oh."

"But I can't kill you."

"Thanks."

"He died?"

"Yes."

"And you've been running things?"

"Yeah."

Saylor sighed. "Your father was a phony."

"No, he wasn't."

"And I'm sure that you also are a phony."

"I'm not."

Saylor went outside. JJ followed him. Saylor walked back to his bucket and turned the water on.

"Why are you dressed up like a bear?"

The water gurgled in the bucket. Saylor turned to him.

"Why are you dressed up like police?"

"What the fuck are you doing?" JJ said. "You're the bigfoot."

"No," he said. "I'm a Shawnee. People can call it what they like."

"You killed a bunch of Kindred's dogs, didn't you?"

"Kindred was lucky I didn't find any of his children that night."

"Jesus."

"Lift up thyself, oh judge of the earth: render a reward to the proud."

JJ shook his head.

"Jack Kindred is gonna kill me."

"Is that right?"

Saylor shut the water off and turned around.

"Help me, Saylor. Help me and maybe I can get you off easy for this." JJ pointed back at the bear on his head.

Saylor seemed to think about this for a moment and then turned the water back on.

"Help me."

"Hold this."

Saylor put the bucket of water in JJ's hands and bent to fill another.

He waited on the other bucket to fill.

"Follow me."

They passed the greenhouses and came to a stable where two horses stood eating, dipping their heads to the hay. Saylor bent down on a knee and pulled a plug out of the bottom of a metal trough letting the old water leak onto the ground, when it was empty he replugged it and poured the first bucket in.

The old man pet the horses with practiced tenderness, whispering into their clockwork ears as they drank. One was a sleek roan with a few spots on its flanks and deep industrial gray points on its muzzle. The other was a greying chestnut with a shooting star blaze on its forehead. The chestnut kept an eye on JJ as it drank.

"What will you do?" Saylor asked.

JJ dug in his pocket and pulled out a little piece of paper and held it up for Saylor to read.

"Elias Road," read Saylor.

"That's where I'm going."

Saylor gave it back to him.

"Help me."

Saylor rubbed the horse's enormous head. Its eyes never leaving JJ.

Saylor draped a blanket on the chestnut and smoothed it.

"You've seen what goes on back there?"

Saylor didn't answer.

"You've been back there, haven't you?"

"Yeah, I've been back there."

"What is it?"

Saylor took a saddle and placed it gently on the chestnut's back.

"You know how to ride a horse?" he asked.

"Yeah," said JJ.

Saylor took the cinch under the horse's chest and thread the latigo snug through the buckle.

"Can you do this?" Saylor said pointing at another saddle on the barn wall.

"It's been a minute."

"How long's a minute?"

"A few years."

"Get out of the way."

Saylor saddled the roan.

"Be good to Sally. She's the easy one."

"So you'll do it?"

Saylor looked off towards the hills and said, "You work in mysterious ways, Oh Lord." He looked at JJ. "Kindred is the latest blossom on a poisonous bush that's been growing for five hundred years."

"Well," said JJ. "Ok."

Saylor grabbed the reins, stuck his foot in the stirrup, and eased his long leg up over the saddle. JJ lifted himself onto the horse and Sally turned and they circled once and JJ sat unsteady.

"It's alright, girl," Saylor said.

The unseen sun was low and cast the clouds with electric edges. They trot to the woods into a tight deer trail. Saylor looked back.

"How far is it from here?" JJ asked.

Saylor, bear head bouncing with each trot, did not answer or turn his attention from the trail. The woods were hot, and the insects hummed like hundreds of electric lights. They rode for several miles in silence. The horses are sure-footed. Soon the moon hung in the sky and the stars began to pierce the darkness.

Saylor spurred his horse through the underbrush, disturbing a nest of lightning bugs, sending tiny sparks all around them for a moment.

"Yonder a mound," Saylor said, pointing through the white sycamore trunks where there grew what looked like a ten-foot belly rising out of the earth.

Along the trail, there were strange markings carved into the trees, petroglyphs of stick figures standing with their arms raised.

"Here." Saylor stopped his horse and JJ rode up next to the old man. He looked an ancient dread, a two-faced nightmare, the marble eyes of the bear shining in the moonlight.

Saylor dismounted and mumbled to the horses. He lent JJ a hand to help him dismount. Saylor tied the horses to a tree and set some feed out for them from a bundle.

"I can't see a thing," said JJ.

"Quiet now. Voices echo in the valley."

Saylor took a torch from his saddle and kneeled at the foot of a rock wall and lit it on fire.

"Which way we headed?"

Saylor stood and climbed up through loose shale to a narrow slit in the side of a rock wall and disappeared inside. JJ got his flashlight out and shimmied inside scuffing against the uneven wall. Saylor knelt at a cave wall, his bear head in the stark shadow of the torchlight. JJ traced a stick man etched in the limestone. On the ground, red faded beer cans with a lion logo on them covered in brown dust.

Saylor disappeared down a narrow passage and JJ called, “Saylor?” The tiny word ricocheted down the cavern. He had to crawl. He could hear Saylor ahead shifting through the rocks. The loose gravel aggravated and stuck to his knees. At the other end, the air hummed. He held his light up but could not see the ceiling or where the far walls began. His footstep echoed.

“Saylor?” he whispered. “Saylor?”

The limestone glared blue in the light.

Saylor appeared from behind a rock ledge. The old man’s face covered with dark dirt. “This way. Forte.” He followed the lumbering shadow into another break in the wall. Water trickled in small rivulets, and a pale fish-skinned lizard darted out of his light into a crevice. The drumming of the drips grew louder.

He tripped and dropped the flashlight, it bounced, went dark, and he listened to it roll across the cave floor to drop and bang down into the cave. He couldn’t see his own hand or feel when his eyes were closed or open. He called the old man’s name again and his voice came back, desperate and hollow and frightened. He felt his pants for his lighter and brought it out and struck it and sat for a moment in the warm light looking at the wet cave wall. The day’s exhaustion came to him. The metal wheel burned his finger and he let go casting himself back into darkness. Seeing nothing, hearing nothing, his father’s voice came back to him, words recorded years ago as he moved around the lonely office with a drink in his hand clinking in the empty spaces.

January 1989

Nelson and I were driving along the old road up near the tunnel. You know, years ago a busload of church folks died in there. That's why they closed it up. There's lots of stories but that's the truth. I sat with an old-timer who was there. He told me every detail. Even had his own theories he called them about sin and hypocrisy and what not... Now, I ain't one for hyperbole or false hopes or superstitions. But it was just dark, and we seen somebody standing at the other end of the tunnel, dressed up like a Union soldier. Had a glimmer, now just a bit, of Glen, my brother, to'em. The way he moved. I know that don't make much sense. Maybe I just seen what I wanted to see, you know. Ghost stories is popular with the tunnel, and it ain't impossible there's a methane leak that builds up in all that concrete, but the thing is, Nelson saw it too. I been back up but ain't seen it again. Nothing but the dark of the tunnel I tell Nelson every morning. No Glen. No church folk. No Union soldier. Just a giant borehole through the rock with a tiny light at the end that I been looking down my whole life.

7

He followed the passage as it narrowed and expanded and emerged from the cave into a deep ditch surrounded by rock walls covered in red clay. The smell of honeysuckle and pine in the air was intoxicating and he breathed it in deeply. Through the trees above him he could see Orion's belt. He found a rocky foothold and stepped up into the Ohio heat, pulling himself up by the tall grass. He stood slick with clay and mud and wiped his hands clean on the grass and looked around to get his bearings. He followed the archer north and found a deer trail. The frogs were croaking in unison and the insects whining around him. He stumbled from the brush onto Elias, a narrow gravel road covered with trees, and set off up the hill.

The moon's thumbnail hung in the dark and the bats shuttered over the stars. He came to a gravel turn-off and followed it down a hollow where he found a Crown Victoria police car parked between a truck and a black Impala. A pile of empty beer cans lay there at the edge of the drive. He crept back to the road.

After a while he came to a burned-out trailer that sat skeletal in the grass, shining bluish and metallic-like a daguerreotype. A charcoal chair lay inside but nothing more.

A mile or more down the road he came to a light that hung from a four by four staked in the ground plugged into a yellow extension cord that led to a grey shed with a corrugated, aluminum roof. Two four-wheelers sat there and he felt how their engines were still hot. Worn wheel tracks in the grass went east towards Jack's cabin. A generator hummed behind the shed. The windows were shuttered, but he could see the slivers of light at their edges. A little further down the road stood a large metal hangar with an enormous aluminum roll door and at its foot a semicircle of large square cages half of them covered in green tarps. A figure moved inside them, and he smelled a strange, rotten smell, like a dog den. He struck his lighter and moved it close to the cage revealing in its small light a black bear. The dark matte hair sticking through the wire grid. It sniffed the air with wet expressive nostrils giving off a quiet mournful puling. In the next cage was another and in the next another. Fastened with huge metal padlocks sitting on cinder blocks, he counted twenty cages. The bears moved painfully slow, reclining, the cages barely large enough to accommodate them. The look in their wet, sad eyes, one of permanent despair. Each had a square of shaved fur exposing their sandpapery grey skin where a clear plastic tube came out of a small round incision. The tube arched down to a liter plastic bottle on the ground outside the cage collecting their sap-colored bile.

Even skin and bones, they weighed hundreds of pounds.

He lifted one of the tarps. Inside a bear salivated a green unhealthy discharge from its slack leather mouth. Another cage was empty, mangy fur and shit on the metal grid.

The shed door opened and light and laughter poured out into the yard. JJ dropped to the ground. Someone approached with a flashlight. JJ waited. They carried a bucket with a ladle. A bear groaned.

"Y'all hush, I got your supper now."

JJ crept around the cages and watched him feed the first bear, slopping a foul liquid into a large bowl. He snuck around to the first bear and approached the man from behind. JJ stepped on a stick, and the figure turned. He rang the butt of his gun off their skull, and they fell stiff. Their flashlight rolled in the grass to stop on a bear face wincing in the light. JJ grabbed it and shined it on the fallen, whimpering man's face. It was Carl Kindred.

JJ's heart collapsed. He knelt down beside him and took his shaking hand. Carl's eyes were open and frightened, and he looked at JJ. He tried to speak and gasped for air; blood gurgled out his nose.

"Carl, Jesus, kid. Carl, can you hear me?" JJ put a hand on Carl's forehead. "It's ok. It's ok." Carl leaned his head down and blood poured out of his ears.

The shack door opened again and another man came out humming. He went to a tree about thirty feet away from them and pissed.

"Carl?" The man called as he was pissing. "Carl? You fed those hairy fuckers? Come on boy, we got another hand to go."

Carl could hear his voice being called, and he spit and tried to sit up.

"Jesus, I'm sorry kid," JJ whispered. He spit blood in JJ's hands.

"Carl?" The man approached them. "What the fuck? JJ?"

"Junior, I didn't know it was Carl," JJ said. "Call for help."

"What the fuck did you do?" said Bullet. "What did you do?" Bullet spotted JJ's gun on the ground and grabbed it.

"Ernie! Ernie, get out here!"

"I didn't know it was him," said JJ.

Ernie came from the shed.

"What the hell is going on?"

Ernie shined his light on JJ and then at Carl.

"You're fucked this time, JJ," Ernie said.

"I didn't know it was him."

"Fuck this," said Ernie. "I'm gonna shoot him."

"No. No. This bitch is mine," said Bullet.

Ernie shot JJ in the chest, and he fell against the cages and sat in the grass next to Carl clutching the seeping hole, his legs spidering.

"Damn, Novak, didn't I just say wait on me? Dammit. I'm the one wants to shoot this fucker. Carl? Carl? Dammit, we gotta call somebody."

Behind them, the metal roof on the shed began to pop and sizzle as flames leaped from the back and dense smoke filled the air.

"What the hell is going on?" said Ernie.

"Fuck, I got my shit in there."

Their silhouettes stood against the fire. JJ sucked air through his clenched teeth. To the east, the other shack was on fire, and they turned to watch the flames dance across the roofline. JJ eased himself to the ground and came face to face with a caged bear. It groaned and moved about excitedly in its cage watching the fire. Something in the hangar exploded and the fire belched out of its high windows. They felt the heat from fifteen yards away. The blackening bone studs collapsed in the first shed. A filing cabinet was engulfed in flames, what might have been a bed.

"It's caught in the trees," yelled Ernie pointing up. Several huge trees caught fast like matchsticks crackling and fizzing.

JJ watched Saylor approach them, the bear head bobbing. He came on steady but in no hurry. Then raised his arms like a horror movie monster. Bullet felt its shadow and looked over his shoulder and dropped JJ's gun. It fired and the strobe roared over him. He doubled over and found part of his ear missing.

Saylor swiped at Ernie's neck and stomach, and Ernie lurched a tentative step forwards and stopped, a look of confusion come over him. Blood welled up behind his hand and poured from his neck. His eyes rolled back in his head, and he fell backward into the dirt, dead.

Inside the dark beast's mouth lay Saylor's crooked nose. JJ thought he saw a look of recognition and acknowledgment there on his face. They watched the hangar roof collapse. Saylor peered down at Bullet pondering the blood on his hands then turned around and took off running down Elias. At some point, JJ had lost his bandage and the pinky again stood upright and out of place on his right hand. A pain he'd not noticed. The tiny lobe of flesh like fishing bait, a grub standing erect as the world seemed dying around him. JJ grabbed his Colt and trained it on Bullet.

Bullet held up a hand to stay him from shooting.

"You see that?" Bullet screamed, unable to hear his own voice pointing in the direction of the murderous bear.

In the distance, a motor whined, and they listened to it approach. A crazed Jack Kindred on a four-wheeler emerged speeding down Elias. Bullet watched him vanish down the dark road then looked up at the burning shacks and knelt down dabbing at what was left of his ear, looking at his hand as if to test whether it still bled or not. Then he sat, and they rested there a moment contemplating the woods burning around them.

8

The sky was full of smoke and haze, bright with the fires. The bear dropped into the dark mouth of the cave; the jagged stalactites glistening like diamonds in the torchlight as he worked his way down into the fetid air. On the cave walls ran herds of stick figure deer. An insect with undulating rows of segmented feet crawled across a mud wall, and the ancient miniature bats hung asleep or dreaming blinking occasionally their blind, obsidian eyes. Jack followed the smudged torch smoke with his flashlight as it had marked the cave ceiling. Bovine points sprouted from his forehead calcifying into hard semi-transparent horns. In a vaulted room, the bear's footsteps echoed. He turned around, holding the torch up, and waited for the red-eyed cow. He came stumbling on the loose rock, scuffing his giant shoulders against the irregular walls, and emerged screaming, running towards the bear, lowering his newly weaponized skull, aiming them at the soft Indian heart. Saylor grabbed the horns, and they went spinning through black space.

I'ma dissect you, Jack hissed.

They rolled through two wooden swinging double doors onto a table where men sat playing cards. Saylor fell back knocking their drinks over and sending the poker chips somersaulting through space, the table tipped and he sat heavy on his ass. Reverend Acuff stood at the table affronted, his head reddening as he rose, mad as hell, working his jaws. He held up his large hands as if to call on God, his massive fingers fluted like some giant gorillas. The queen of clubs sat speared on one of Kindred's new carbuncular nails. Saylor pulled himself to his feet. Kindred shoved him down a red hallway lined with taxidermied ducks lit by lanterns. The green shag carpet soft on Kindred's boots. The horn pierced Saylor's hand, stigmatic in the tendons of his palm bleeding, he recoiled and tapped the great bull with his fist in its bugged eyes. On they squabbled through fields of constellations flipping through a groundless space and coming, at last, to land on JJ's cluttered desk breaking through the foam office ceiling tiles. They knocked the portrait to the floor where it fell face down. JJ pulled his gun but the cold machine turned hard in his hands, shapely and geometric, but as if carved from a marble imitation, its levers useless. He watched them scuffle and felt himself just a small player in his own dream, impotent among their stampeding around the office, knocking the plants to the floor and the books and the papers and the flag tossed in the air in the crisis of their angry two-stepping.

Of this at least I am certain, said Saylor. *The world will break free from your grip a thousand more times.*

JJ thought at first he spoke to the horned beast, but Saylor was looking at him. They lit out the back door and in a multidimensional drift, like a series of puzzle pieces separating, the fabric of space tore. The bear changed into Owl, a grainy atomized magic, for a moment both creatures coexisting there, then this new bird, lifting itself on massive wings. Kindred the raccoon holding to the Owl's back feathers as they flew up and came crashing back into the mouth of the cave. They splashed into black waters and the torch fizzled and rose to the top as they sank into a depth dark and darker, lost in a rising confetti of bubbles. The Owl with its wings open sinking, air pouring from its open beak and the drowned raccoon descending, its eyes dull in death, hands up in supplication, the small spiked mouth open forever.

At the bottom lay rich loam, heavy with years of undisturbed decay, out of which lovely plants would grow, new plants to choke the living without remorse, without ambition or hope, plants that would raise up new creatures with wild, violent hearts and songs that no man would hear.

When it reached the calm waters of the Ohio River the face began to dry in the sun. Two crows settled on the chest and started working at the tongue and the open eyes. Carp followed nipping at the swollen fingers. It passed under a railroad trestle and smacked one of the concrete struts with both feet, disturbing the crows that flew up, cawing like mad. It veered to the side and coast lengthwise, pitching like a log. The crows circled and came back. They settled again on the chest and worked at it until all the exposed flesh was gone and the body's clothes hung in tatters in the current, stretching out behind it into the muddy water.

Made in the USA
Columbia, SC
12 May 2025

57850516R00100